EVERLASTING
FIRE

MAYA DANIELS

By Maya Daniels

Infernal Regions for the Unprepared

Black Hand

Lower World

Everlasting Fire

Place of Torment

Vinci Books

vinci-books.com

Published by Vinci Books Ltd in 2025

1

Copyright © Maya Daniels 2023

A CIP catalogue record for this book is available from the British Library.

Paperback ISBN: 9781036706616

Chapter One

Life was all about cycles.

Ups and downs of a rollercoaster ride where the only way to survive is to buckle up and hold on tight.

Or, scream your head off.

I truly believed that I knew that, but it always took one more kick in the kidneys that buckled your knees to drive the point home. On a good note, when the knees hit the ground there was no other option left but to go up.

I kept telling myself that.

One day, I might believe it, too.

Forearms resting on my raised knees, I watched the metal bars of the cage with dispassionate detachment of a lost soul. Was I lost? No, definitely not. At that point I had more things I cared about—people that counted on me—to simply give up. I still owed it to myself to stay adrift if only just for a while, and finally face everything I'd discovered and all that was taken from me.

The strangest thing in it all, something that kept

returning in my mind, was that the one place which haunted my every nightmare, or waking hour, didn't affect me as expected. Maybe I should've said not as bitingly as I thought it would. The terror was there, deep in my psyche like an insistent insect prodding, buzzing.

I simply ignored it because if I focused on it, it would've driven me insane.

Clammy skin and a quickened heartbeat along with the shivers crawling up and down my spine served as a reminder of my predicament. The cages were not a place anyone would easily forget. Not even an Atua. But, the thought of Alice and Dominic out there alone and targets for my enemies was more frightening.

Samir better make good on his word and look after them.

I knew I was too good of a prize for the Syndicate to pass when I surrendered so the rest could get away. Foolishly, I told the shifter to come for me. It sounded smart at the time when I said it because all I wanted was to send him away and keep him alive.

As I sat in the cramped space between the metal bars, I realized my mistake.

"I never thought I'd see you here again," a familiar voice rasped from somewhere in the darkness. The harsh whisper was too loud for the silence around us. "I should've known you'd be back. No one leaves this place for long."

After a few years, I had thought I'd never see the hell hole again, but I didn't vocalize my rebuttal. The voice succeeded in reminding me that you never truly left this place. The rancid stench of body odor, dried—or fresh—blood along with the moist soil squelching under the feet of the patrolling witches, was permanently absorbed in our skins to torment our every waking hour. My eyes adjusted way too easily to the barely visible stone walls, embracing the dull light which was hardly above the flicker of a dying candle. The memory fed on our fear like a leech sucking the life out of us.

I'd used that voice many times as an anchor to ground myself to life while I struggled to stay awake, bleeding all over the packed dirt. It whispered tales of worlds and people that didn't exist, just to torment me more and force me to stay alive. In those times I loathed it and was grateful for it, too. I never remembered the words, but the tone? I'd recognize that tone anywhere.

"Nostalgia." My shoulder rolled in a blasé shrug while I picked on my chipped nail. "They made me feel so at home here, I was starting to feel sentimental for the familiar stench as a free person out in the world." The voice hummed part in disbelief, part in amusement. "No one wants to see me all sappy, or slobbering all-over the place, so I had to come back. Me crying is a horrible sight, believe you me."

"You should've done everything to stay away. Things have changed down here from the last time we spoke. The witches are dying," the person whispered dejectedly, but before I could ask more questions it fell silent. I felt the person distancing themselves like a physical push to the chest.

For so many years, I heard the voice cajoling me to hold on, to not give up, yet I never saw the face it belonged to. I thought they didn't want to be alone and in some twisted sentimentality did everything to prolong my suffering by talking until I opened my eyes. They were in a cage just like me because I heard the clinking of the metal bars every time the person shifted, yet I had no idea if it was a male or a female. To me, it was just a raw rasp, a tone that never allowed me to find peace in death. Only the darkness prevented me from coming face to face with my tormentor and savior.

It was nice to see the Syndicate gave me back my old cage though. How very thoughtful of them. At a closer inspection, I did recognize the tiny space which had been my home for too long. The scratches left in the hard-packed dirt where I sat were also familiar. I left them there while I was writhing in pain on many occasions.

"Someone's comin'," the voice hissed.

That was when I heard the scuff of shoes on the ground. Soft, but not nearly silent enough for my next-door neighbor or me. My shoulders tensed as I subconsciously reached for the dagger on my thigh, finding an empty sheath. I curled my fingers next to my leg and stared ahead, acting as if nothing was amiss.

"You truly are a sight to behold, Brooklyn." Frederic emerged from the dark void as a dim light bloomed into existence from behind him.

Eyelashes fluttering, I blinked rapidly from the sudden light in the pitch black of the space until I brought him into view. His long hair was falling loose around his shoulders, the platinum color turned orange from the torch flickering behind his head. Ominous shadows were cast over his high cheekbones that made his eyes look sunken into his skull and his perfect face resemble an angel of death. Dressed in an immaculate suit, the Council member stood out like a sore thumb in the pits of hell he created for the rest of us. My gaze dropped to my feet so he couldn't see the hatred burning there.

"The service is impeccable here, as always." Keeping my voice light, I smiled coquettishly at the ground, but he saw it. Frederic missed nothing. Rage was coming off him in waves, strong enough that it was difficult to breathe. "The care they offer makes me glow from the inside. I'm assuming I have you to thank for that, Sire?" Calling any of them Sire bubbled acid up my throat, one I had to swallow down.

"I will take great pleasure in breaking you." There was nothing remotely humane in his promise. Which was loaded with anticipation, judging by the slight tremor in his voice. "I didn't have nearly enough fun the last time you were here."

"I'm looking forward to that." My eyes slowly lifted so I could peer at him through my lashes. He had enough self-preservation to take a step back when my lips curled and the smile turned wicked. The reaction pleased me immensely which made him livid. "Should we start now?" I purred.

Frederic moved so fast I had no time to twist away from his grasp. The magic the witches had woven into the bars of the cages sapped my strength until I was as good as a human in a fight against him while surrounded by the metal bars. He took hold of the collar of my shirt in his fist and yanked me hard against the metal, mushing my face between the bars.

"You think you can stand against me, child?" His breath washed over me when he got in my face. "Just because I like toying with you, it made you think you can win against me?" My body shuddered in revulsion when his tongue poked out and he licked a trail up my cheek. "It's been too long since I've had your blood." The murmur shriveled my veins because I was sure I wasn't meant to hear it.

It brought memories of fangs ripping into my arms and thighs as I was too busy being delirious while my life flashed and flickered in front of my eyes.

So many times.

Too many…

"I wouldn't dream of it." My words were muffled by the cage biting into my skin, but I had to keep him talking. If he decided to feed, there was no way for me to get away without tearing my neck open. "Only a fool would dare think they stood a chance against you."

"Precisely." Shoving me away as if I disgusted him, he glowered down his nose at me when I slumped on the dirt. Stroking their egos worked no matter the situation. "Now, let us talk about our dear friend Samir."

Crawling on my hands and knees, I tucked myself in the narrow cage as far away from his reach as possible. My reaction earned me a chuckle that I wanted to punch from his face. Unfortunately, my prison was only tall enough to sit in and just wide enough to move a couple of feet to the left and right, which meant I had to wait for my chance. I'd been shoved here for a few days already, and my muscles were sore from lack of movement. It was crazy to hope they forgot about me, yet I did, until this ass showed up.

"What about him?" Keeping my eyes locked on his, I wiped the cheek he licked with a grimace. "You miss him already?"

"What did he tell you?" He folded his hands at the small of his back before flaring his nostrils. "And don't lie to me, girl. If you don't tell me the truth, your life means nothing to me."

"He said I'm the most beautiful Atua in existence, and he has been secretly in love with me my whole life." My eyelashes fluttered as I coyly curled my lips. "Can you believe it?"

Angering Frederic was a dumb idea.

It didn't stop me from doing it, but I found it necessary to acknowledge the fact even if it was just to myself. My kind could smell a lie. Well, the more powerful of us could, but my experience in the pits of hell taught me how to bypass it somewhat. I might have been inexperienced in the matters of the heart thanks to Johnathan and his betrayal, but I wasn't an idiot. I knew Dominic liked me, so I kept the way he looked at me when he thought I wasn't paying attention firmly in mind as the lies spilled from my lips.

Frederic frowned disapprovingly at me.

"You lie." He spat it like a curse, and even the witch holding the torch behind him flinched. Luckily for me, doubt was riding his tone hard.

"Am I though?" Tilting my head to the side, I focused on the witch.

The male had the hood of the robe lying flat on his shoulders, exposing his face to me. Sunken cheeks formed dark shadows on it over the sigils swirling there, but his shrewd eyes were tracking my every word. Back when I spent all my days in this place I feared those like him. Now, with the information I had, I had to wonder if I could recruit their help.

On its own my hand lifted, reaching for the pendant that was no longer there, but I caught myself in time. Spearing my fingers through the clumps of unbrushed hair I tugged on the strands to untangle them. Let Frederic think I was vain, as long as he kept his hands and fangs to himself.

"It's astounding. You really think you will survive this a second time." Unease prickled the back of my mind at the delighted glint in his irises, but I pressed my mouth shut. Crouching down so we were at eye level, he cocked his head, the long strands of his hair spilling over his shoulder. "Tell me, Brooklyn. How far do you think I need to go until you break? We already know the limits that will bring you to the edge. All I need to do is push just a little when you are there."

"To what end?" I was truly curious. "What makes you think I'll be of any use to the Council if I'm broken? I might turn on you at the end."

"Ah, but you already did turn on us, did you not?" He traced one of the bars with a fingertip while eyeing me as a lion would eye a bloody steak. "For that, you must be punished."

It wouldn't be the first time and I knew his punishments well enough. There was something in the way he said it though that sent a shiver through me. Years of pretending not to be bothered by their insanity and depraved ways served me well to keep my heartbeat calm, but my mind was a different matter. My mouth formed words I had no reason voicing out loud.

"Punished how? What is it you think you can do that you haven't done before?" His growing smile chilled me to the bone.

"I wonder if the shifter would enjoy watching me feed on you." The fangs grew longer as he spoke, and my heart stilled in my chest. "Do you think it'll please him if I do it from your neck, or from your thigh." His gaze raked over me, pausing over my breasts and my pelvis although it was hidden from him with my curled-up legs.

"I'd definitely try the thigh, if I were you." The witch sucked in an audible breath at my answer. Even Frederic's eyes widened at that. "I bet that will rile the shifter up like nothing ever would."

"We shall see." His eyes flashed with eagerness as he stood and strolled away, taking the light with him.

I breathed a sigh of relief.

Dominic was too smart to be caught by the Council, I

had to believe that. But if the worst happened and they brought him to the cages? Taunting Frederic that I was looking forward to feeding him from my thigh was the smartest way of getting Dominic and me out of the hell hole. Because for Frederic to reach my thigh...

He had to unlock the cage.

Chapter Two

"Get up." The bars of the cage rattled as something smacked hard against them, and I gasped as I woke.

The magic keeping me contained must've forced sleep on me because the last thing I remembered was taunting Frederic. After he left, I stewed in my anger, thinking of all the ways I wanted to slice him up the first chance I had my hands on him. Rubbing the sleep away, I squinted at the flickering flame on the other side of my prison and the witch glowering impatiently at me.

"Put these on." Metal clanked and jangled at my feet when he threw something at me.

Twisting around, I reached for it, only to end up dangling shackles from my fingers. Sigils were painted on them and I didn't need to ask to know they'd keep me docile when outside the cage. In the face of my reality, white noise filled my ears.

"I don't think so." I threw them back at the witch.

"Put. Them. On." He snarled each word and hit me on

the cheekbone the second time he flung them through the metal bars.

The side of my face smarted, but I bared my fangs at the ass. "Why don't you unlock the cage and come put them on me yourself?" My fingers itched for the dagger, but I curled them into fists.

"You are only making things harder for yourself." His huff told me I was acting childish. I disagreed.

"Look around you." My hand flopped to the side, pointing at the darkness and everything I couldn't see in it. "It doesn't get harder than this."

"Put them on, I just need to deliver you to the Gulley. We will both be punished if I don't." He waited with a furrowed brow. You'd think speaking to me like to another living being was a foreign concept.

My heartbeat stuttered.

Faint memories tried to push to the front of my mind but no matter how hard I tried I couldn't recall them clearly. My time at the cages was fuzzy in details but made up for it with dread and terror every time I closed my eyes. At the mention of the Gulley, my skin became soaked in cold sweat and my hands begun to tremble.

I searched his narrow face but didn't detect a lie. Without my abilities I wouldn't leave this cage if it was anyone from the Council, but the witch was not that big of a threat by any stretch. I might not be as fast or as strong with my powers muted, but I had fangs. No magic could take those away from me. If the witch tried anything, I'd just rip his throat out.

Gingerly, I picked up the metal and secured it around my wrists.

The door of the cage clinked open the second I was bound, and it swung outward with an ominous shriek of a dying dinosaur in the quiet. The witch smoothly stepped aside and waved his hand for me to crawl out of it, which I did with a lot of muttering under my breath. My muscles were screaming when I unfolded to my full height from the lack of proper circulation, and I stumbled into him. The male steadied me with a firm grip on my arm but didn't protest otherwise as I expected him to do. It allowed me to prod for information while I had a chance.

"What's at the Gulley?" Keeping my tone conversational, I rubbernecked to see if I'd notice something familiar in anything that was revealed from the flickering torch he clutched like a lifeline.

"Death," he told me gloomily.

Whimpers, soft cries, and sniffles were like ghostly whispers haunting everything around us. The stench of wet soil, old congealed blood, and excrements drenched the air and made it pungent enough to be tasted on the tongue. I breathed through the mouth so I didn't empty the contents of my caved in belly and didn't dignify his answer with a comment.

Of course it was death. What else would the Syndicate have hidden in the underbelly of the city. The scuffing of my boots over the packed dirt just drilled it home better. I chose to think of the people that got away and were safe somewhere instead of what was waiting for me. The Council had me to entertain themselves, so maybe they'd leave them alone now. Unfortunately, Samir was with the two I wanted to protect and that made my hopes only wishful thinking.

Any witty comments I had for the witch felt unnecessary.

We reached a tall wooden door after what felt like forever, but I had some exercise so I didn't complain.

Docilely, I stepped to the side and waited for the male to unlock it. It opened to another barred door. That one clanked and screeched loudly as he pushed it inward before he nudged me with the back of his hand to enter it. The moment I stepped through, it slammed shut at my back, pushing me to whirl around on the witch who stayed on the other side of it.

"Give me your wrists through the bars," he ordered, his gaze darting around. "And try to stay alive for a while longer. Don't make them risk everything just to find you dead."

I narrowed my eyes but did as he said, and with a wave of his hand, the shackles fell to the ground. We stared at each other as I memorized his face. Unlike most of the male witches who were bold enough to display the sigil tattoos all over their skin, he had extremely short but still visible dark hair. Most noteworthy, however, was the strange color of his eyes. They were so light green it was almost like looking at shards of glass, not irises of a living being. The male was a bit more muscular compared to the rest, but I couldn't tell if my assessment of that was true because of the flowy robe he had draped over his shoulders.

My body came alive now that the suppressing magic was gone, so I had no time to say anything when he scooped the shackles up and closed the wooden door in my face. Alone, I rolled my shoulders and turned in a small circle, wondering what to do. It was a long hallway with a faint light at the end and nothing else. Moist stone surrounded me and the stench of moss assaulted my nostrils.

At least my abilities were back.

Whatever this place was there was no magic around it apart from the metal door. Pointing my feet toward the faint light, I cautiously headed in that direction. My fingers wiggled in the pocket of my pants, and I breathed a sigh of relief when they brushed against the pendant. In the cage, I didn't know who was watching, so although I could feel the stone there, I didn't dare check.

"Here she is." Frederic's voice set my teeth on edge the moment I entered the illuminated area.

Excited murmurs reached my ears, and blinking rapidly, I brought the vast space into focus. Dread filled me in a tidal wave, and I wished I could unsee it. Atua filled the space around the room above my head, all of them leaning hungrily down to see me better. Isiah and Frederic were lounging on throne-like chairs in the middle of them, dressed to perfection while I stood at the edge of what appeared to be an arena.

My fists clenched. "Why am I here?" My voice boomed and bounced off the high ceiling.

"To earn your keep." Frederic grinned at me with a sadistic jubilation and waved at someone I couldn't see.

All my senses became alert when a ferocious cry of a beast blasted my eardrums a second before a furious creature joined me from the opposite side of the flat dirt. My lungs shriveled when it rose on its hind legs and shook its head. I wanted to say I'd never seen anything like it, but the memories my mind normally hid from me said otherwise. At least two heads taller than me, the creature could've passed for a wolf in another life. What stood a few yards from me was a wolf ripped in half and the two parts were connected by a humanoid form—as if a human grew inside the beast and ran out of space so it split it in half while it continued to expand.

Pitch black eyes with no pupils locked on me, and it roared so loudly the ground under my feet shook violently enough to make me stumble. Its jaw, as long as my arm, was opened wide enough that I saw its tonsils.

Dread petrified me, and I stiffened.

The packed dirt trembled when the beast ran for me. First on two legs then it dropped and loped toward me on all four. Instinct took over and my muscles loosened as I placed all my weight on the balls of my feet.

I waited, my eyes locked on the monster drooling for my blood.

All the noise dwindled in the back of my mind, and I could hear everything about the creature. Each thump of its heart, every scrape of the claws when it pushed off the ground, the breath sawing in and out of an elongated snout. Nothing but me and the creature existed.

It pounced from a few feet away. Just as it was about to snap razor-sharp teeth on me, I ducked and rolled away under its belly to jump back up on my feet behind it.

My own claws and fangs burst out.

The beast shrieked an outraged cry as it smacked hard into the metal bars and skidded to a stop. I didn't wait that time and with a running start jumped on its back. My claws sunk into its shoulders, but my attempt to rip its head, or the throat at the very least, failed. Thick fur filled my mouth, my fangs closing around it with no purchase.

A scream was torn from my chest when it reached back and shredded the skin on my arm and shoulder with five-inch claws. Its massive upper body swung frantically as it attempted to shake me off, but I dug my own fingers further in and squeezed my thighs around its torso. When I was certain I wasn't going to be flung like a dirty rag, I pulled one arm back behind me and, angling it right, I stabbed the claws in its side. They slid smoothly in the human-like skin, and it shrieked a second before black blood gushed from the wound.

Atua were hooting and cheering around us, their joy like acid burning my insides. The moment of losing focus cost me. Tipping to the side so I could reach the skin instead of fur didn't give me as good of a leverage as I hoped. The beast twisted unnaturally around and plucked me off its back like I weighed nothing. I scrambled to grab a hold of its arm, but my blood coated hand slipped over the fur and the creature pitched me to the side.

I sailed high and managed to turn in the air just in time to hit the ground on my hands and knees instead of my back or head. The impact jarred my bones, and I bit on the side of my tongue, filling my mouth with my own blood. One of my fangs pierced my lower lip, and I snarled in pain. Packed soil rattled under my palms when the beast thundered over it to reach me. I had no time to stand up, so I stayed kneeling in front of it.

Putrid breath like decayed flesh slapped me in the face as its jaw opened wide. The creature was about to literally bite my head off, and my own roar of fury mixed with its insane roar of victory. At the last minute I made my move. My hands snatched the open jaw in a bruising grip, and adding everything in me, I yanked in the opposite direction, placing all my body weight into it.

The breaking of bone and tearing of muscle was too loud in the deathly silent arena. Hot blood sprayed me from head to knees and the scream of the beast died down so suddenly it made my ears ring. Gasping for breath and trying not to vomit, I let the broken jaw of the creature fall off my limp fingers and searched the crowd for Frederic and Isiah.

I locked my gaze on them through the blood dripping down my face.

"Impressive." Isiah's slow clap echoed around the large space in the silence, but all I could see was him tearing out Veronica's heart.

Panting, I rose to my feet. "Is that all you've got?" I already heard the second beast snarling from the other side of the arena.

Arrogantly arching one eyebrow he brushed silky hair over his shoulder with elegant fingers. "I'm just getting started, Brooklyn. So eager to die, just like your friend. I'm very pleased." Frederic chuckled next to him like the mention of Veronica amused him.

"You are just getting started?" Repeating the question made them smile indulgently at me.

I grinned back.

"So am I."

With that, I brushed all thought about the second creature away and sprinted for the wall separating the Council members from the arena.

Chapter Three

Arms pumping, I ignored everyone else but the two monsters that hid behind pretty faces and charming smiles. At first, both of them stayed sprawled over their tall chairs, smirking down their noses at me. When I started flinging Atua out of my way right after I climbed the wall as if gravity had no hold on me, shouts and pointed fingers became necessary.

The past collided with my present and something in me just snapped.

After a couple of days, I stopped counting how long I was caged, but seeing the now dead beast brought many things into perspective. Biding my time was no longer an option since there was no way I'd survive long, this time around.

This was not a punishment, or entertainment for the two males.

It was a drawn-out execution.

For one: the Council enjoyed their power too much. The pain they inflicted on others fed them more than the blood they stole from unwilling humans as well as whoever got on the wrong side of what they wanted. They'd go to great lengths to stay where they were, no matter the cost. Veronica was a pure example of that.

I was the second.

Two: the other two people I cared about were only going to stay safe—that was still a great if—as long as I was alive to entertain the masses. Judging by the expression on the Council members' faces, that would be a day longer, two at most. After that, not only were they in danger, but I wouldn't be around to assure their survival. Or at least help them any way I knew how. Dominic, as well as Alice, proved to be very resourceful all on their own. It was just nice to feel included for once instead of being the loner.

And three: I really wanted to be alive and see the Syndicate destroyed with my own two eyes. That thought was like a punch to the stomach and it made me reckless.

Guardians spilled from two sides through doors I hadn't noticed until I was almost on top of the Council members. Swords and daggers left their sheaths as the hissing sound of metal leaving leather called me out for my stupidity. The plan that sounded brilliant moments before suddenly had as many holes in it as Swiss cheese. But it was too late to back down.

I was committed.

Using the crowd against them, I dodged left and right, shoving frantic people at the bare-chested Guardians as I continued forward. A blade bit into my skin, slicing it open when I didn't twist away from it fast enough. Burning pain traveled up my right arm, numbing it to the shoulder. It took a long moment before warm blood spurted out, letting me know the wound was deep. Deep enough to kill me, were I a human.

The loud noise of shouts and screams lessened just as I reached the elevated platform where Isiah and Frederic stood shoulder to shoulder behind four Guardians. As intimidation tactics went, a pretty impressive one, but I was beyond caring. Hunger for their blood was my only goal fueled by the burning in my veins that started with the inflicted wound. What better way to feed it but to destroy the one place that made the Syndicate feared.

The cages.

Fangs bared I ripped into the males with teeth and claws like a female possessed. Taking advantage of my smaller, slimmer build, I ducked, turned and bent at awkward angles to avoid their weapons and to cause as much damage as possible. My right arm was useless, but if I jerked my shoulders sharp enough, I could fling it at them as a distraction. Two Guardians fell with an astonished expression permanently etched on their faces while their lives spilled through the ripped skin on their thick necks.

The beast I left down in the arena took my example like I expected it to, and charged at anything that moved, giving me as good of a backup as any. The Guardians seemed undecided which one of us to fight. Most of them chose the creature, luckily. The handful I was left with fell without causing me too much harm.

"Now, we can start," I told Frederic when there was no one standing between us. I would've preferred the other asshole, but that monster was out of my reach.

Much to my delight, the beast was carving his way too close to Isiah and the second Council member was a bit preoccupied.

"I was hoping you'd do something to warrant your death, foolish girl." Frederic's angelic face twisted into an ugly mask not many survived to remember. His power was pelting my skin like tiny needles while his eyes glowed and stared me down. I'd pretended long enough that he could subdue me with his mental ability so my smirk caught him by surprise.

I attacked.

My fist passed by his head close enough for me to feel his face near the knuckles but not to touch it. Frederic's platinum hair billowed wide as he spun around my body and kicked me in the spine. I hit the throne-like chair face first, and tucking my knees up I hugged it so I could keep my balance. The wood cracked ominously, but it didn't break.

A fist wrapped around my hair and yanked my head back hard enough to crack my vertebrae, as Frederic's hot breath brushed the overheated skin of my neck. I pushed back off the chair with everything in me, forcing the Council member to lose his balance and go down under me. We hit the ground hard, the edges of the wide stairs biting against my ribs until bright lights blinked at the corners of my eyes. Stone cracked and spiderwebbed under us, leaving a body-shaped hole in it. After we stopped rolling, I kicked away from him and scrambled to my feet, keeping Frederic in sight but searching for the creature as well.

The beast was munching on Guardians to our left with Isiah trying to get close enough to kill it. Unlike the first one I'd ripped apart, this one kept swinging its long arms, holding everyone far enough away from its body. Frederic was on his feet, and I had to focus on him, but I saw the creature sway on its feet and my heart hammered against my bruised rib cage.

Time was up.

"I'll enjoy killing you." Frederic spat at me, blood dribbling from his mouth. I almost laughed, seeing that the fangs had split his lower lip. "Or, I'll keep you in my chambers a while to watch you suffer."

"I will die first." Searching for an opening, I inched to the side, refusing to consider why he'd keep me in his private rooms.

"That can be arranged." The words were barely out of his split lips when he pounced.

Unfortunately, I was already unsteady on my feet and my head was filling up fast with cotton. Unyielding hand snatched me by the neck and my feet left the ground before I saw him move. Long elegant fingers tightened until there was no way for me to fill my burning lungs. With my right arm hanging limply by my side, I clawed at Frederic's hand with my left while he laughed at my pathetic scrambling. Insanity lurked in the depth of his ancient gaze while he held me like a ragdoll, my legs kicking weakly in the air.

Fading fast, many thoughts brushed against my mind but none long enough to grasp. My claws met the bone of the Council member's hand, yet he didn't release his hold on my throat. Instead, he tilted my head to the side, ready to bite. Bile burned and churned in my stomach.

A feral cry exploded in the almost empty arena.

It made Frederic flinch and twirl around to see where it came from. His grip slackened as he took me with him and we both saw the black panther headed our way at an impossible speed. Green eyes lit from somewhere within burned with disdain aimed at the male holding me like a puppet. Seeing the feline as the bigger threat, Frederic lobbed me away from him.

I landed in a heap, coughing and sputtering as I fought to endure the rapid healing of my windpipe. Rubbing my tender neck, I pushed the hair out of my face in time to see the Council member and the panther collide. Everyone left standing, including Isiah and the creature, were flung like rags when the air blasted outward from the two males.

Gulping oxygen on pure instinct, I swung wildly when someone touched my shoulder. My fist hit nothing, but I was flipped over and flopped on my side with a grunt. Samir's face popped above me, concern etched on his features.

"Brooklyn, stand up." Tucking his arm under me, he didn't wait for me to obey. "We need to get out of here."

"Dominic." My rasp earned me a disapproving scowl.

"He is fine, unlike you." His caramel skin looked paler than usual, the dark goatee standing stark against it.

"You should've seen the other guy," I muttered and for some reason wanted to laugh. The numbness in my injured arm reached the shoulder blade, spreading down to my side. I was burning from the inside out.

Samir's lips twitched, but the smile slipped too fast. From where he cradled my limp body on his chest, I could see the creature swinging at Isiah. But the Council member was winning. Black blood poured from too many places on the beast. The panther and Frederic were tearing at each other on the other side, leaving holes like craters everywhere they rammed at each other. When my focus was not on murdering or the two monsters they planned for me to fight, the rest of the arena revealed itself and everything inside me stiffened.

Bodies were ripped apart and tossed everywhere. The ground, the walls, including most of the seats were filled with corpses and everything reeked of blood. So much blood. Noticing where I was looking, Samir tightened his arms around me while my fangs throbbed painfully in my gums.

"Hold tight, I'm getting you out of here." He turned to

run with me curled up like a youngling between his arms but stopped in his tracks.

A handful of Guardians spilled from the door to our left, the one Samir wanted to use for our escape, with a few witches in tow. The male that shackled me was among them, his strange eyes finding me instantly. The glass-like gaze flicked to the panther momentarily before it returned to me. Dazed, I wondered why his hands didn't glow red like the rest of his kind, when his words returned to me and snapped me out of the fog.

"And try to stay alive for a while longer. Don't make them risk everything for nothing."

"He knew." I mumbled to Samir.

"What?" My father's friend frowned down at me but returned his attention to the witches spreading around to block our escape.

"The witch." It was barely above a whisper. "He knew you were coming. He… he told me to stay alive."

Samir's head snapped down and his gaze bored into mine. Vaguely, I pondered whether I'd said something wrong, but it was there and then gone. I did see him turn his head to look at the panther with some sort of respect—which made no sense—but I could've imagined it.

My body and mind were on fire.

That was when magic burst into life, the low chant of the witches humming powerfully in the vast space. The Guardians stood behind them instead of attacking.

"Can you stand?" Samir shook me to get my attention.

"Not well enough to be of help. There is something wrong with the cut on my arm." The words slurred.

"Poison." He snarled viciously.

I ignored him. "If you hold me on the side, you can use me as an extra arm. Just not the right one."

"You can barely keep your eyes open." Samir sounded distracted, and I followed his gaze to the cloud of red magic forming ahead of us.

"I can still kill." Struggling to force him to put me down, I breathed a sigh when my feet touched the stone. "I looked worse the first time I crawled my way out of here."

"That you did." He smiled at me proudly, the expression tightening my chest. "When I tell you, drop down and flatten as much as you can. The magic will fly high, they're aiming it at Dominic."

"No." Flailing to shake him off, I almost fell backward.

"Look." He rattled my bones before subtly pointing at the witches. "The shifter will be fine."

The male witch with strange eyes was waving a different spell. A dark yellow, like burnt gold, and he had it turned toward the panther. Whatever blood I had left curdled in my veins, but it was too late. The spell burst from his fingers and wrapped around the panther in a bright almost orange bubble. My breath caught, but the shifter didn't stop fighting. His powerful body continued to coil, twist, and turn as he slashed at Frederic. The Council member seemed disheveled for the first time since I'd known him. Blood crusted his expensive suit.

"Brooklyn, down."

Samir yanked me so hard I dropped like a rock over the uneven floor, my chin smacking hard on it and jarring my teeth. Flattening as much as I could, I was pretty sure I didn't breathe as the spell zapped above me, scorching strands of my hair as it passed. The arena severely shuddered, rearranging my organs as it rocked under me.

Isiah shouted something at Frederic, but it was drowned under the ceiling crumbling on top of us. Blocks of rock crackled and plummeted down all around, billowing dust everywhere when they slammed on the floor. All I could think about was *'not again,'* remembering Alice's kennel when Johnathan destroyed it. A scream lodged in my sore throat when I was bodily lifted off the floor and draped over something muscular, smooth, and very much alive.

"Move." Samir snapped from above me and my good arm wrapped around my transport as Dominic loped with incredible speed toward one of the exits, me draped over his back like a saddle.

Feeling the male under my touch even in his animal form loosened something inside me and, eyes closed, I held on tight, trusting him to get us out of there. There was someone else running with us too, not just Samir, but I didn't dare look. I hoped it was the witch and not one of the Council chasing us. My entire world was spinning and I had only enough energy left not to fall off of Dominic's back.

It lasted for a while; my death grip on the shifter. Too soon, the numbness from my injury spread wide enough that my arm slackened its hold and I felt myself slipping off the muscular back.

Darkness took me before I hit the ground.

Chapter Four

DOMINIC

"She's still bleeding." Unnecessarily I made that clear, although all of us could see the blood pouring out of Brooklyn's arm.

My heart was a wild thing in my chest, pounding hard enough to knock my ribs loose.

The wound was a clean cut from the back of her upper arm to the crease of her elbow, and I was shocked the blade used didn't take her arm off. It came close, but she must've moved out of the way just in time, much to my relief. The edges of the skin which gaped open were swollen and bruised, refusing to fuse back together no matter what we tried. The injury looked angry, taunting me for our inability to do anything about it, while the female thrashed on the bed, burning up with fever. Her red hair was almost black from the sweat pouring out of her, sticking to the overly pale skin of her face and neck. Her complexion was naturally pallid but it lost whatever little color there was to it from the poison Samir kept mentioning.

Her kind did not get sick.

They either lived or died.

The pummeling organ in my chest lurched violently.

"Fix her," I spat at the witch kneeling next to the bed while he watched me with wide fear-filled eyes. "Now."

"I'm trying my best, Dominic, but nothing is working." His washed green gaze searched my face. "I've never heard of a poison like this being used in the cages." His puckered face turned to the female. "Not that they told us much of anything," he muttered under his breath.

"Somebody must've said something." My roar rattled the tall windows as my shoulders hunched and shook while I loomed over him. A glass of water that sat on the bedside table tipped over and shattered on the gleaming wooden floors. "Think!"

"Raging and intimidating the help won't do anything good, Dominic," Samir said on a sigh while the air vibrated from the volume of my shouted words.

Shoulder propped on the wall, the bloodsucker had his arms crossed over the silken shirt he wore, one ankle crossed over the other and a disapproving twist on his face. While I felt like scratching out of my skin, tearing his expensive looking mansion apart along with everything in it, the arrogant male appeared bored. The shift rode me hard. My animal was pacing under muscle and bone, stretching me beyond my limit.

"I'm not your butler, prick." The witch glared at the male. "I'd like to see where you'd be if I didn't risk my neck back there."

I couldn't blame Rowen for bristling at the insult. The witch risked his life more than once to help me bring the Syndicate down after we came face to face on one of my self-appointed missions. Instead of attacking or bringing attention to me, he hid me and had been helping me ever since. I never bothered to ask his motivation, and he never divulged any personal agendas or details. If I needed help, all I had to do was leave a sign for him to meet me and he would provide what was in his power to aid me. It suited me just fine, but I should've known it wouldn't be enough for the Atua. Machiavellian by nature, the former Council member did not disappoint.

"Why did you?" Suspicion laced Samir's tone. "Why are you here instead of wagging your tail at your masters?"

"You were one of his masters until a week ago, Samir," I bit off through grinding teeth. "Let him work."

"Rub it in, why don't you?" Rowen flattened his mouth. "Insanity overrode my good sense, that's why I painted a target on my forehead. I should've left you all to die in that hole."

"What is the correlation between the two of you?" Straightening, Samir moved closer to the kneeling witch. "I might be overly cautious, but you must understand my distrust of your kind."

"You had no distrust when I led you out of the cages." Not backing down, the males scowled at each other.

I'd had enough.

"Stop bickering and fix the female before I rip your spines with my bare hands and feast on your still beating hearts while you watch." My quiet, even tone made them both jerk their heads in my direction.

"That's oddly specific." Rowen cleared his throat and fidgeted with the folds of his robe. "Right, well. All the spells I know are not working." Avoiding my glare, he turned wisely to Brooklyn.

"We all know what needs to be done." Samir pressed a hand on the mattress to lean over her, and smoothed away some of the hair sticking to her cheeks. My fists clenched and the bite of my claws poking out was the only thing that stopped me from flinging him at the wall. "We need either a sample of the poison, or one of the blades they've used it on."

"I'll get right on that, as soon as you find a way to bring me back to life after they rip me limb from limb." The witch grumbled in frustration.

This was getting us nowhere, and the human wasn't even in the room to drive us insane. Samir sent her to finally get some sleep since she was literally bouncing off the walls and screaming at us the whole time we were coming up with a plan to save Brooklyn. If I hadn't seen it with my own eyes, I never would've believed a human could survive on tea and no sleep for close to seven days.

"How long can she survive bleeding out like this?" My question came through numb lips. I didn't want to hear the answer.

"I don't understand this." It was Samir that spoke. "Unless they used a specific dagger, her father's to be precise, nothing should do this to an Atua. But if that were the case, they would've killed her. That blade never misses its mark."

I already knew all of that. Before I even checked, I knew that the dagger was no longer in her possession, but that cursed night when she gave herself up to save the rest of us, I'd seen her use it. The question was did the Syndicate have the weapon or was it somewhere in that alley where she fought them. Twice, I went back to search with nothing to show for it.

"How long, Samir?" Impatience was drilling a hole in my gut.

Forehead scrunched up and lips pursed, he blinked at the oozing wound. "She won't die. I should say she's not supposed to die an ultimate death while her heart is still inside her, but she's also supposed to be able to heal instantly from an injury like this. If everything progresses as normal for our kind, not taking the poison into consideration... In a few days the body fluids will seep through her pores, and she'll go into a sleep until she heals."

"But we don't know if she'll wake up." It wasn't a question.

I could hear it in his tone that he wasn't sure if she'd ever open those soulful, haunted eyes of hers. The ones that made the blood race through my veins every time she gave me her full attention as if she could reach in and grab hold of my soul. The very idea of never seeing the fire in her irises when she spoke of those that wronged her, or the curl of her rose-colored lips every time I narrowed my gaze at her, sent a chill so deep in my bone marrow that gooseflesh covered my arms. To ward off the feeling, I wore a track in the floor with my pacing.

Samir locked his dark, phantomless eyes on me. Sorrow lurked in their depths, crushing my lungs like a fist. "No, we do not."

My fist connected with the wall booming a sound and my arm embedded into it to the elbow. Dust and pieces of plywood billowed and rained down on my face and shoulders while I snorted air through my flared nostrils like some raging beast. Images of my dead parents, of my sister's unseeing eyes, mocked me in my mind's eye. No matter what I did, I could never protect anyone from the Syndicate.

Not my family, and most definitely not Brooklyn.

"Dominic." The witch tried calling my name but my fists rained on the wall in fast succession until the hallway on the other side of it was revealed. "Dominic!"

"Can you keep her in the same state until I bring down a sample of the poison?" Samir drawled at Rowen over the rumpus of the rapidly crumbling barrier between the rooms.

"How can you be so apathetic? She gave herself up for us, including your pathetic excuse of a life." Whirling around, I bellowed at the male, bleeding fists trembling and clenched at my sides. "Look at her. Look. At. Her!"

Arching an eyebrow, Samir sneered at me. "If you stop acting like the animal you are, you'll see that regardless of the blood loss and the fever, her heartbeat is normal. We don't know if that will change, but I assure you, tearing down the house won't help Brooklyn. So, unless you intend to collect yourself and help come up with a plan, I suggest you leave. Go…run or something. Chase a rabbit." He said it with a grimace and a disgusted flick of his wrist.

I bared my teeth at the male.

"Both of you are not helping." Rowen started to say, but a faint sound, barely above a whisper, drowned his voice out.

"Dominic?" Brooklyn's murmur had me next to her before my name fully passed her lips.

"I'm here." My knees crashed on the floor and the rasp came off broken from the heartbeat thrumming in my throat. "How do you feel?" Slamming my mouth shut, I gnashed my teeth to stop spitting more bullshit out. What kind of a dumb question was that?

Samir and Rowen lingered behind me, their presence while the female was weak driving my protective instincts berserk. For Brooklyn's sake, I shoved them down and reached a shaking hand to brush her clammy cheek. Her eyelashes fluttered, but her eyes stayed open.

"Did I die?" Her soft, husky voice slayed me.

"No." It came out harsh so I forced myself to calm down. "And you're not going to. You hear me?"

"Then… why?" Swallowing thickly, her tongue poked out to wet her dry lips. "Why do you look like a ghost?"

It took me a moment to notice the twitching of her mouth and the humor in her tone. Her emerald eyes—similar, yet darker than my own—glittered feverishly on her pale face. The knot squeezing my lungs unraveled its hold and an unbidden snort burst through my nose. Brooklyn's gaze kept dropping to my neck as she struggled to stay awake.

"I was redecorating for Samir." I could do this. She needed me to lighten the tension and I'd do it if it killed me. "His interior design tastes are outdated."

"I'm sorry." One tear rolled from the corner of her eye as she whispered her apology before she latched onto my neck.

My whole body stiffened when the fangs popped my vein like a grape but her warm mouth suctioned, and instead of pushing her away I found myself holding the back of her head while she fed. At the back of my mind, something prodded to get my attention, the fact that when I'd offered before she took my wrist instead of my jugular, yet I couldn't move away. Everything in me responded to her lips on my skin, and I melted into her until dark spots blinked behind my closed eyelids. Samir was shouting something behind me that I couldn't hear until strong hands grabbed my shoulders and yanked me away from the female feeding on me.

"That's enough." The male stepped toward Brooklyn with a stern scowl on his face.

It all happened too fast.

All signs of her fever gone, Brooklyn snarled and leapt at Samir, fangs bared. Rowen yelped and scrambled away when the two collided, but I was too lightheaded to get off my ass and help. The male threw her off him back on the bed, but she was up before hitting the mattress, slashing her claws at him. All the blood I had left curdled when I saw her green eyes flash as red as her hair. She wasn't upset that he pulled her away from me as I thought, she was trying to kill him.

Gathering what strength I could I called out. "Brooklyn."

Her face snapped in my direction and the color flickered between green and red in her gaze. The other two males were saying something but my focus was on the female. I saw the horror and torment in her irises before they hardened into that of a predator, and with one long look, she threw herself at the windows, shattered one of them and disappeared into the night.

"What just happened?" the witch whispered breathlessly.

I stared unblinkingly at the last place I'd seen her.

"They didn't use poison," Samir hissed, tearing at his hair. My gaze snapped to him. "They used contaminated ancient blood. We kept it under the pretense that we were guarding it. I should've known Isiah and Frederic would use it. I'd seen its effects only once and dared hope to never see it again. She's not dying, Dominic." A new kind of dread dropped like a rock in my stomach. "She's mindless in bloodlust. Nothing will squelch the thirst she feels. All she'll do now is kill."

Kill, kill, kill.

It kept echoing in my head on repeat. Strangest of all was the fact that the deaths didn't bother me as much as they should've. What sent a bolt of fear through my heart was the fact that it would break Brooklyn if she ever came out of it.

I had to find her.

Chapter Five

ALICE

"What do you mean you lost her?" My sock-clad feet whispered over the polished floors as I moseyed to the couch. "Brooklyn is not a button that popped off your shirt for you to lose her. She's a person."

No one can dispute the effectiveness of strong black tea, stolen chocolate that the boys thought I'd never find, and pure determination after the last week or so. How I didn't pass out in that time was anyone's guess but just thinking about what Brooklyn was going through kept my eyeballs wide open. The moment my head hit the pillow, however, after Samir told me to either sleep or he would knock me unconscious, I was out like the dead. The result of my slumber was a skull numbing headache, fluff instead of a brain and fur stuck to my teeth although I did brush them. Twice. The wolf had a bad habit of getting in my face while he slept on my pillow like a damn house cat.

"Brooklyn is not well, Alice." Dominic struggled to talk to me without glowering or growling. I could tell.

"Did you not see me standing there when the two of you brought her back? Well, three of you, but I still don't know who the freaky guy is." Frowning at him, I lowered my cup of tea on the table with a thud so I could rub circles on my temples. "I know she's not feeling well. What I don't know is why I can't go see her or why you're saying you lost her."

The truth of the matter was, I barely had enough energy to reach the living room or there was no way they would've stopped me if I wanted to see my friend. The guys might see me as a pesky human but I turned into a trash panda with rabies to get things my way. It was the only way to deal with these supernatural brutes. Plus, Brooklyn had threatened Dominic with pain if anything happened to me. I used the shit out of that to my advantage every chance I had.

"She's lost to bloodlust." Samir's burr washed over me like a bucket of ice-cold water.

"I'm sorry, what?" I jerked upright where I was slumped on the couch, startling the wolf at my feet. His ears flattened and he barked viciously at the tall, lean man who was watching me from an unsmiling face.

Not man, Alice, vampire. A voice in my head reminded me. The vamp must have been trying to scare me, so I stayed where I was. Next thing you knew he would be forcing me to eat, I had a feeling it was coming. Women clawed our way up in the world to have a voice and be equal to men. So far, the supernatural were quite behind on that front with all their chest pounding, guerilla tactics, and manhandling they had going on.

With a nervous laugh, I snatched the tea off the table and took a long sip. "I'm drinking this tea, and then I'm going to see Brooklyn. The two of you can stay here and chat, so stop trying to come up with stories. They won't work."

"He is telling the truth." Dominic seemed pained by the admission. "After Brooklyn attacked me when she woke up, she escaped through the window." All my blood solidified into ice. "I searched the city for her but lost the scent eventually. You woke up shortly after I returned."

Not bothering to comment on that, I plonked the cup with a slush of black tea all over the table and my hand, and darted out of the large room. My socks slipped and slid over the polished wood and I stopped myself from headbutting the walls a few times by slapping a hand on them until I reached the room where I'd left my friend. Bursting through the door, I shrieked when I found a robed figure hunched over the bed before remembering the weirdo they brought with them in the house. At my scream, Dominic filled the doorway at my back like a messenger of death.

"Where is she?" When he just stood there, glaring at robe dude, I punched him in the chest and hurt my hand in the process. "Where is Brooklyn?"

"I told you human, are you deaf?" Glowering at me, Dominic flicked his gaze over mine. "I lost her."

Early morning was splashing through the parted curtains and the sun streamed over his face. That was when I noticed the torment there and his words replayed in my mind. He wasn't pissed off at me for asking questions, he felt guilty that he couldn't find her.

From the day I met Brooklyn I admired the woman with everything in me. She was my hero for flipping a metaphorical middle finger at an organization everyone feared, smiling as she did it. I wanted to be like her. To make her and myself proud. Little rough around the edges, socially awkward and distrustful, she reminded me a lot of my late father. No one understood him, but he was one of the kindest and most loyal people I'd met, just like Brooklyn. While the world called them insane or monsters, they were just different.

My dad with his conspiracy theories.

Brooklyn with her fangs.

My heart hurt for my friend and I had every intention of finding her, but it shattered to pieces at the expression on Dominic's face. The guy was surly and too proud for his own good, maybe a little damaged, but from day one, I knew he cared about my friend more than he let anyone believe. Seeing him barely holding on to his sanity just confirmed what I already knew as fact. That was one of the reasons why I made it my mission to get the two of them together.

The second being that I wanted my friend happy.

Brooklyn didn't think she was worthy of love.

I disagreed.

"Okay, so we just need to get our heads together and figure out where she'll go." Awkwardly, I smoothed the t-shirt on his chest where I hurt my hand in a dumb attempt to hit him. Were shifters built from steel in their world?

"You should go to one of the reservations as we discussed beforehand." Grabbing me by the arm, he propelled me down the hallway. "I'll find her."

Rubbernecking, I twisted in his hold to see the robe dude staring at us from the open door we left behind. "What about the scary monk guy?" Dominic glanced down at me as I dug in my heels on the floor, but he only dragged me along since the stupid socks slid over it. "Who is he?"

"A witch," the intimidating man told me without inflection.

"Wait, what?" Wiggling like an eel out of water I tugged

and twisted until he released his hold. "Why didn't you say so sooner. Maybe we can help." My glasses dropped to the top of my nose and I shoved them back up with a forefinger to better frown at Dominic.

"We?" He gave me an impressive raised eyebrow that I could never pull off.

"Yes, we. You said the robe dude is a witch." Huffing, I waited until he cautiously nodded at me. "He is a witch, I am a witch. We can try to do some spell to find her."

"You're not a witch," he deadpanned.

"Says you." I dodged when he grabbed for me and skirted in a wide arc to get away from him. "My records prove otherwise."

"Your record of using Brooklyn's blood to almost kill yourself to open a magical circle and the breadknife someone else spelled with which you almost killed us?" I was in half mind to shave his eyebrow while he slept.

"When you put it like that, it sounds awful." Hiking up the rolled-up sweats Samir gave me so I could have a shower, I shuffled a few steps to stay out of his reach.

The hallway was littered with low stone columns, half of them filled with abstract art pieces the rest with vases full of blooming flowers all of which cost more than my entire life earnings. No matter their cost, the sweet cloying smell was worsening my headache with each breath I took, adding to the nausea churning in my belly.

"The human can do magic?" Robe dude ambled further away from the doorway, his tattoos coming to life under the light streaming from the dangling crystal chandeliers. There were no uncovered windows anywhere in the huge house apart from the room behind him.

"A little," I rushed to say before Dominic could destroy

my only chance to help find my friend. "I only just started, so I'm rusty and clueless on most things, but I learn fast."

"I wonder if there was a witch in the family." Head tilted to the side, he stared me down with eyes so light in color they were unnerving.

I pushed the glasses up the bridge of my nose. "Who knows, both of my parents didn't get along with their families well. Like this once, when I was in middle school, my mom took me to my second cousin's birthday party and two minutes after we walked through the door there was drama galore..."

A scream cut off my story when Dominic used it to sneak up on me and snatch me by the arm. The wolf who was patiently waiting by my side snarled at my shriek but one glower from the shifter and he tucked his tail. What a useless animal. When I least expect it he will act feral and go nuts to protect me, but at moments like this he was the most incompetent wolf I'd met in my life. Holding onto the sweats so I didn't lose them while I practically had to jog to keep up with Dominic's long stride, I glared at the animal.

"I don't know why you won't let me try." Sounding breathless from lack of stamina despite all the running for my life I'd been doing lately, I huffed my annoyance. "Do you have a better idea? No? I'm so glad you said that because let me tell you, I do. If we try a tracking spell, we might find her."

"Stop talking nonsense, human." He wouldn't slow down or look at me until robe dude spoke from down the hall.

"She can do a tracking spell?"

"No, she cannot."

"I can if she would assist me." Dominic swung around

to face him so fast he almost flung me into a wall. "Can she really do magic?"

Holding my breath, I stared at the stubborn man who was manhandling me. Reluctantly, with a monster frown scrunching up his forehead, he bobbed his head. "Around Brooklyn she could a little, yes."

"Let us try, then." The robes billowed around him when he rushed back toward the room. "I think her scent has changed, that's why you lost her. This might work." He disappeared through the open door.

"Don't try anything stupid, human." Dominic glowered at me. "I don't wish to explain myself to Brooklyn if anything happens to you. Am I clear?"

"That's the spirit." Beaming brightly at him, I yanked my arm out of his grip. "You already know I'll find her with a tracking spell."

My socked feet were sliding toward the opened door before I was done talking.

"Have you attempted something like this before?" Dominic trailed after me.

"Nope." I hiked my sweats up and grinned at him over my shoulder as my glasses slipped to the tip of my nose. His face became instantly blurry. "But I've watched all the seasons of Charmed seven times. I've got this."

A string of curses followed me to the room as I bolted there before he could catch me.

Chapter Six

DOMINIC

"It is worth a try," Samir pondered under his breath.

On Brooklyn's orders, he told me everything, including the alleged prophecy, and I could see his calculating gaze pinned on the human. I didn't need Brooklyn to tell me to keep Alice's gift a secret. The male might have been helping, but until he proved that he could be trusted with something like that, I debated the wisdom of the situation.

I needed to find my female, not fight to protect the human.

My female? I'd ponder on that later.

"Humans dabbled in magic throughout history." Swathing my unease in disinterest, I rolled my shoulder in a shrug. "Rowen is strong enough to pull this off on his own. I think he is humoring her. Alice was adamant she was going to help find her friend."

Slogging up the rolled-up sweats, the human shuffled around as she helped the witch set up bowls and crystals around the basement Samir had suggested we use for this spell. She looked ridiculous with pants three times her size paired with one of Samir's button-down shirts, but you couldn't tell if it bothered her by the way she was focused on every move the witch made.

"It would appear Brooklyn does inspire loyalty in others with ease," the male murmured, eyeing me from the corner of his eye.

"Not being a piece of shit does that, yes." Stretching my lips wide in a humorless smile, I focused on him. "You'd be surprised what you can inspire when you don't murder indiscriminately."

"We've been at this many times, Dominic." He blew an exasperated breath with a disappointed shake of his head. "Things aren't always what they seem. Sometimes you simply must play the hand you are dealt the best way you know how."

"If her father was alive, would you be able to say that same thing while you look him in the eye?" I didn't need to know Brooklyn's full story to piece enough together from the little bits and pieces she shared. The guilt twisting Samir's features said I'd hit the nail on the head.

"Maybe I could've done some things differently were I to go back in time." On a sigh, he rubbed the back of his neck. "Alas, I cannot, but I did keep her alive. That was all that matters."

Having nothing to say to that, I clamped my mouth shut. That was more than I could claim I'd done so far, same as when it came to my family and to those under my father's roof to whom he offered safety. Protective instincts or not, everyone around me ended up hurt, or eventually dead. The female was no exception. If it weren't for me or the human, she never would've gone to that hell hole I found her in.

"I cannot read minds, but whatever you are thinking, it

does not look good," Samir mused with a halfhearted chuckle. "Brooklyn is a fighter, Dominic. It'll take more than bloodlust to take her down."

"I don't want to know what can take the female down, I need to know what can cure her." Pushing the words through clenched teeth, I shook off all the thoughts of death and family. The burden was crushing my chest as it was, no need to be brought up to the surface.

"If she didn't attack you first, I would've said nothing." Leaning back on the wall, he rolled his head to the side so he could look at me. "When our blood gets tainted to a point to elicit bloodlust, an Atua is put down. Insanity eats at our minds fast enough that no one ever bothered to find a cure for it."

"How long does she have?" I asked with my throat tight.

"As I said, I would've said hours at the most. But, just like with everything, Brooklyn is an exception to the rule for this as well."

My hand was wrapped around his shirt, and I lifted him off the ground before he finished talking. Shoving him harshly at the wall, I snarled in his gloating face. "Stop talking in riddles or I will kill you."

"She released you." Samir was not smiling, but I could hear it in his tone. It pissed me off that he didn't try to defend himself. "In bloodlust she should've torn your throat open, but she didn't. When I forced you back to get you away from her, she actually released the bite. I've never heard of such a thing happening before. She should've been mindless, but..." His shrug was awkward, yet he did it masterfully.

With effort I lowered the male back on his feet. Replaying the moment in my head, I took a couple of steps away before I changed my mind and ripped his heart out while it was still beating. Brooklyn didn't bite viciously to begin with like I would've expected from a mindless predator the way Samir explained it. Weak and dazed, I should've been her first victim out of the three of us, yet she stood between me and the two other males. Attacking the stronger so she could protect the weak, that sure sounded like my feisty female, not a mindless killer.

"Ah, I see we are on the same page now." Samir nodded more to himself than me.

"Her eye color flickered before she burst through the window." My breathing accelerated and my heart pounded against the roof of my mouth. "She's fighting it."

"Just like she tackles everything else in her life. Brooklyn is her father's daughter. As I told you, she is a fighter, but we still need to act posthaste."

"If you two love birds are done touching each other, I think we are ready to start," Alice hollered from the other side of the basement with a cheer that matched the drumming of my heart.

"I think I like the human." With a low chuckle, Samir side stepped me and tugged his shirt to flatten the wrinkles I'd made on it when I yanked him off the floor. "Let us see what magic can tell us that we cannot find out for ourselves."

"If you think you know where she is, why didn't you say anything?" With a fist propped on her hips, Alice glared at the male.

"I have assumptions, human." Hands raised at his sides in surrender, he cocked his head curiously as he sauntered toward her. "If you heard what Dominic and I discussed, it's only logical to assume she will hunt down those she sees as a threat."

A rock dropped at the pit of my stomach. "You think

she went back?" If I could have lifted my feet to move, I would've throttled the male. Lucky for the cunt, my legs were a solid unmovable stone where I stood.

"The cages?" He glanced over his shoulder, smoothing the damn goatee in thought. "I think not. I was thinking more in a way of hunting our kind through the city. Maybe that's why you lost her trail."

It made a weird sort of sense, but it was all based on wishful thinking at that point. For all of Samir's jabbering he did give me an idea that—although good—seemed very much improbable. I still had to ask, if for nothing else, to at least remove it from the list I was jotting down in my head.

"Even if the tracking doesn't find her, I will." Conviction was clear in my voice, enough to raise Samir's eyebrows to his perfectly formed hairline. "Rowen"—ignoring the pompous ass, I pinned the witch with my glare and searched his owlish gaze— "can you reverse the poisoning when I bring her back?"

He gaped at me as he crouched next to the circle made of salt. "Reverse... the poison... if I can reverse it?" the male stuttered, blinking a million miles per second.

"Seriously, Dominic, you guys need to dial down a bit on the staring daggers scale around here." Alice rushed to the witch and patted him on the head the same way I'd seen her do to the fucking wolf. "Are you trying to make him have a heart attack or did you intend to get him to pee in his robe. Gee, intense much?"

Rowen stiffened the moment her hand landed on his nearly bald head, but in less than a breath his shoulders dropped and were no longer up to his ears. My eyes narrowed as I watched the human calm a witch like he was a pet as if it were the most natural thing in the world.

"Don't mind him, Rowen," Alice murmured as she

crouched next to the witch, not missing a beat as she petted. "Dominic just hisses like a snake ready to bite, but deep down he is as cute and cuddly as a kitten."

I bristled while Samir grinned from ear to ear. Fucking prick.

"I'm not afraid of Dominic," Rowen grumbled, stealing glances my way around the mess of Alice's hair. "I know he won't hurt me because he needs me."

"He won't hurt you because Brooklyn will feed him his yam sack for breakfast even if he doesn't need you. I was beyond tired when you guys brought her back, but I remember hearing you helped a lot with the rescue." Shooting a pointed scowl over her shoulder in warning, she gentled her tone and my chest felt tight. "My friend sees things like that as worthy of returning the kindness. And, Dominic is not that much of an ass. He huffs and yowls to keep people away from him. Right now, he is worried sick about Brooklyn and that's the only way he knows how to show it."

"The cat references are getting old." I griped begrudgingly, and avoided Samir's intent stare.

Alice blinked at me. "Oh." Pushing her glasses up with a finger, she smiled bashfully. "I didn't want to insult you if I used some other animal accidentally so I made it a point to only use cats for analogy."

Rowen barked out a laugh.

"Sorry." Rowen removed the human's hand where she was still petting him on the head and squeezed it gently in gratitude. "I never thought I'd live to see the day when someone would compare Dominic to a cat and live to tell the tale." He pointedly avoided me. The witch wasn't as dumb as he looked.

"Pfft," Alice waved him off and stood up, dusting her

knees, although they never touched the ground. "He is grumpy as I told you, but you should hear him purr when you scratch behind his ear…"

"Start the spell." She squeaked at my snap and glowered at me over the rim of her glasses.

"You'll be in big trouble for scaring me like that, just you wait." Her finger shook when she pointed it at me.

Muttering things under her breath that I pretended not to hear, she shuffled to the position Rowen assigned her. The witch looked at anything but me while fighting the need to grin like a fool. His grimace made it seem he was constipated. I scowled at both of them with my arms folded across my chest when Samir saddled up to me shrouded with expectant air.

"I do not purr." My grouchy comment made the male snort.

I was going to kill the human.

Chapter Seven

DOMINIC

"Why is it taking so long?"

After an hour I scuffed a track on the floor with my pacing. Fists clenching and unclenching at my sides, I had to move or I would've killed one—or all of them—in the damn basement. The vast, almost empty space reeked of ozone and expelled magic with nothing to show for it apart from the melted candles, a few cracked crystals, and the pungent smoke of herbs burning in multiple bowls around their circle.

Rowen started them off with a simple chant that the human followed easily, progressing steadily to more complicated incantations that made my head hurt and my tongue thicken from the harshly spoken words even though it wasn't me saying them. Alice held on like a champ, her velvety tone hitching on a few mispronunciations, but otherwise she held the wave of Rowen's smooth melody in synchronization that shouldn't have been possible.

The buzz of their voices abruptly stopped.

"It's not working." With a weary sigh, the witch swiped

the sleeve of the robe over his glistening forehead. "I found some of her hair on the pillow which I used to specifically target her, but it's only circling around the industrial part of town. No precise place, or even a street."

Rowen glared at the clear crystal dangling above a map in the middle of their circle with hatred borne out of hours of laboring over it so he could make it move. It didn't even twitch, which elicited the unflattering comments the male didn't voice, but ones I could easily read on his face.

"If I had her blood, it would've had more strength. Like this…" His hand flopped in frustration at the map as he trailed off.

"The sheet was drenched in her blood." I followed Rowen's glower to a sheepish Samir.

"I thought I was doing a good thing." The Atua male threw his hands in the air. "Dominic was losing his shit, what would you have me do? Leave the evidence of how badly she was injured for him to stew over so it can push him over the edge to try and kill us all?"

"Where is it?" Alice jerked her sweats up as she shuffled away from their circle. "I'll run and grab it, let's not argue, my headache is killing me."

"I washed it. The same way I cleaned out every drop she spilled when we carried her inside." Samir shrugged with a weird expression on his face. "He can smell it other-wise. How was I to know you'd need it? You." He stabbed an accusing finger at Rowen. "You should've thought of it before. It's all your fault."

"I'm stuck in a house full of supernatural cry-babies," Alice murmured and rubbed at her temples through the fabric of the sleeves that had swallowed her hands.

"The human needs to rest. Magic takes a toll, and she

overtaxed herself." The witch stomped toward her and took her face in his hands to check for something.

Alice slapped him away. "Hey, no touchy, magic dude. You don't see me lifting your robes to check if your testicles have dropped, do you?"

"Why would you ever do that?" Rowen angled away from her with a horrified look on his tattooed mug.

I had enough of their bickering.

"Is blood all you need so we know where she is at all times?" I barked at the witch who was warily eyeing the human.

"Yes," Rowen gulped and tugged the robe closer around him. "A few drops for a spell should do it. If we need to repeat it daily, then a few each time."

"Stay here." My feet were already pointed at the stairs that would take me to the main level of the mansion. "I'll bring you the blood."

"You lost her trail, remember?" Alice called at my back. "How would you find her?"

"Rowen said the spell keeps circling over the industrial part of town." Reaching the stairs, I took them two at a time and already had a plan of where to start. "From what Samir told me, I'll just follow the trail of dead bodies to her."

"I'm coming with you." Samir spoke from behind me when I stepped into the corridor on the first level.

"There is still daylight left outside which will make you useless to me." My boots thudded over the winding stairway that led to the room assigned to me.

After our escape the Atua male insisted we stay at his home that no one but him knew existed. With zero options left on the list of places to hide, Alice and I accepted the offer. Samir regretted it an hour later when he realized the wolf would be staying with us, too. The wolf felt the hostility from the male immediately, so he'd been marking every damn corner of the huge house.

"I'm old enough to withstand the daylight." Unperturbed, he followed my every step. "Taking her blood however is all on you when we do find her. She wasn't particularly happy to see me when I faced her."

"That should tell you to stay back." I slammed the door in his face.

Yanking a drawer open, I snatched the first t-shirt I could reach and changed the one sticking to my back that stunk to high hell of burnt herbs and magic. After I kicked off the boots, I did the same with a pair of jeans, wondering how Samir managed to find clothing for me but left the human to slouch around wearing his shirts and sweats. After stabbing my feet back into my footwear, I rushed to the bathroom and shoved my head under the faucet to wash off the odor from it.

"You need another set of eyes or she'll have you chase your tail." Samir continued the conversation the moment I opened the door as droplets of cold water dribbled in my eyes.

That's when it hit me.

"You feel obligated to help because you washed the blood off the sheets." His chagrin told me I'd guessed correctly. Shaking my head and spraying water all over him, I shouldered my way out of the room. "You'll just get in my way, Samir. If I need help, I'll call."

"Brooklyn is my responsibility, Dominic. Whatever it is that you two have, keep it out of my sight." My back hit the wall toppling one of the vases full of flowers to the ground. It shattered at my feet, spraying blooms and water everywhere. "I am going." Samir sneered at me with one hand firmly planted at the center of my chest.

Everything in me screamed to unsheathe my claws and punch them inside his chest where I could shred his heart. It must've shown on my face too because the male stiffened and his power blasted out of him in a tidal wave. My upper lip curled from his lack of control but something about his dark gaze gave me pause. It wasn't just guilt that pushed him to insist on accompanying me.

Samir was afraid.

If that fear was for the female or for himself remained to be seen.

It made me step back and rethink killing him in his own home. I could use another set of eyes even if I didn't want them. To keep the peace for now, I gave him a sharp jerk of my head in confirmation.

"Stay out of my way."

His hand dropped and together we jogged to the garage where a fleet of vehicles lined up from wall to wall. Most of them were covered with some sort of cloth, but a couple waited to be used. Samir darted for a muscle car at the front of all others, but I beelined for the motorcycle I saw calling my name.

"Hey, Dominic?" Samir shouted from the side, and I turned my head to grin at him. "Catch."

Something sailed through the air, and on instinct, my hand jerked up to snatch it before it smacked me in the head. Cold metal bit into my skin as I palmed it only to find a set of keys when I uncurled my fingers. I glanced from them to the bike and back at the male.

"I had a feeling you'd want to jump on it the moment you had a chance." With a small curl to his mouth he ducked inside the car and a second later an engine purred like a waking beast in the closed space.

Still grinning, I reached the sleek black bike in two strides and threw my leg over it. A deeper purr joined the first when I turned the key and a thrill passed through me when the motorcycle vibrated underneath me. Twisting the throttle a couple of times, I flicked the stand with the heel of my boot just as the door rolled up ahead of us.

Samir zoomed out of the garage like the hounds of hell were chasing him.

I was riding his ass until we reached the open road.

The male might have been much older than me, but he ate my dust on our way to downtown Chicago.

Chapter Eight

ALICE

"Are they gone?" Staring expectantly at Rowen, I bit my lip so I didn't chortle in his face for tugging his robe closer when he saw me watching him.

"I believe they are, yes. Why, human?" His eyes narrowed, and he took a step back. "They'll be back any moment, you know."

"Are you actually scared of me?" Gaping at the witch, I could see the truth written all over his reddening face. "Oh, my god, you are."

Slapping my thigh, I laughed so hard my glasses slipped from my nose. In all the crazy going on, if anyone had told me a supernatural being would be afraid of me, I'd have told them they were nuts.

"Don't be absurd." Rowen glowered at me. "I don't want to accidentally harm you in any way and then need to explain myself to Samir or Dominic. As long as you keep your hands to yourself, everything will be fine."

"You have nothing to worry about, I'm leaving anyway." Snickering under my breath, I snatched some of the bowls and candles to put them away. The sooner we cleaned up, the faster I could go and do what I needed to get done.

"Leaving?" Forgetting all about his apprehension, he shuffled toward me. "I don't think that's a good idea. If they find the female..."

"Brooklyn." My murmur made him trail off.

"I beg your pardon?"

"Her name is Brooklyn, not female. She has boobs and a vagina, we know she's a girl." His mouth opened and closed a few times while I glared at him. Yanking on the bottom of the shirt Samir gave me to wear, I used it to clean up my glasses because if I kept looking at him, I'd chuck them in his face. "I don't know if any of you are aware that you twist normal words to make them sound like insults."

"For calling her a female?" Confusion scrunched up his face. "She is a female." Like I needed his confirmation to know that. What an idiot.

"She is, and she also has a name." All of the earlier frustration reared its head so I turned it on him. "We have fought hard to be seen as equal, and just when I honestly believed we made some headway, I get plunged into your world and have to listen to you men talk about us as if we are weak and useless. Whatever would we do without you brutes to protect us or tell us what to do."

"Males." Rowen frowned at me as he searched my face which was as red as his had been a moment ago. When I side-eyed him he rubbed a hand over his overly short cropped hair with a sigh. "We are males, not men. None of us are human. And we don't use those words as insults, it's just how we talk, I guess." His shoulder twitched in a shrug.

"Yeah, well, maybe you shouldn't." Jamming my glasses back on a little too hard, I had to blink to get rid of the tears stinging the back of my eyes when the frame hit hard on the bridge of my nose.

"Why do I have the feeling this has nothing to do with how we talk to and about each other?" Prying the few candles I carried in my arms, he set them aside and planted himself to block my way. "This is what I think. You want to do something that you shouldn't and to stop me from preventing you, you're starting an argument."

"If I want to do anything, you can't stop me." Mimicking his pose, I folded my arms across my chest.

"I'd have to disagree, human." An arrogant smirk curled his thin lips. "There are many ways I could stop you, I just hope it won't come to that."

The wolf who was curled up in a corner up to that moment raised his head and bared his sharp teeth at the witch. Jumping up and rustling his fur, he padded menacingly across the room until he reached me, not turning his gaze away from the robed guy.

"And I hope whatever magic you plan on using, you can call it up faster than he can clamp his teeth on your neck," I told him conversationally. "That lady they are looking for might be just a female to you, but she is my friend. So, you're going to stick around here and do what you normally do while I go to find help."

Rowen sucked in a breath to argue, no doubt, but the wolf snarled, effectively shutting him up. With a thin smile, I petted the animal on the head in gratitude as I backed away from the witch without taking my eyes off him. The guys would be gone for a while, but I had no time to waste in explanations. Not that I wanted to tell the witch where I planned on going.

Reaching the stairs, I whirled around and bolted up as fast as I could while holding onto my sweats. When no footsteps could be heard behind me, my heartbeat slowed down. First stop was Dominic's room where I ruffled through his drawers until I found a belt. The vampire made sure to find Dominic clothing that fit but left me with stuff made for giants so I had to get creative. After wrapping it to hold my pants up, I snatched a long-sleeved shirt too. The weather was getting colder and I had no idea how long I'd have to stand outside.

The shifter accidentally gave me an idea on how I could help. I switched out the button-down silky shirt for a much warmer top, and with the wolf on my heels, I tiptoed around the massive home until I reached the garage. My fingers curled around a set of keys hanging on the wall, and I moseyed around the collection while pressing the key-fob to check which car they belonged to. The thing beeping looked more like a UFO than a vehicle, so I made two trips until I ended up with a long sedan. It didn't appear like a cheap car by any means, but at least I wouldn't owe the vampire for three generations if I scratched it.

Opening the back door, I waited for the wolf to jump in before inching forward with one last glance around the silent space. As soon as I slipped inside the driver seat I screamed bloody murder and dropped the keys on the floor.

"For fate's sake, human. Why are you screaming?" Rowen snapped from the passenger side.

Eyes bulging out and the glasses barely holding on to the tip of my nose, I gasped for air and kept my heart inside my chest by firmly pressing my hand there. Since I'd left him in the basement my neck had developed a kink from craning because I'd wanted to make sure he wouldn't see me. How in hell did he get inside the car I'd had no idea I'd be taking?

"You scared the shit out of me." Gulping air, I glared at

the useless wolf on the back seat through the rearview mirror. "Thanks for alerting me there was someone in the car."

The yellow eyes of the animal stared flatly at me with zero apology in them.

"How did you know that I'd be using this car?" Avoiding Rowen's gloating, I ducked to search for the keys I dropped at my feet. My fingers fumbled with the slippery keychain for a bit before I was able to grab them, and just for a second, I lost myself in the fantasy of using them to stab him in the arm.

"I didn't, I just used a cloaking spell to follow you." As if this was an outing with a friend, he tugged on the seatbelt and clicked it on with an excited grin.

"You're not coming with me, Rowen. Get out, so I don't waste time." The engine rumbled like a beast in the closed garage as I adjusted the mirrors. "I have a long drive to reach the Bad River Reservation, someone has to stay to tell Dominic that I'll be back."

Samir's home that he so graciously offered us to stay in was about an hour outside of Chicago. That left me a good five hours, give or take, to get to the closest reservation. It wouldn't have been my first choice, but Bay Mills in Michigan added close to two hours on top of that and time was of the essence if the guys found Brooklyn as they hoped.

"Shamans?" Rowen hissed and reeled back so hard the back of his head smacked the door. "You said the female was your friend. Are you trying to get her killed?"

"What I'm trying to do is help her, and you are holding me back. So, if you'll please get out of the car, I'd appreciate it." My gaze darted over the dashboard and above eye level until I spotted the button I was looking for, and jammed it with my thumb in glee.

The door of the garage groaned as it rolled upward.

"I'm coming with you." Stubbornly, the witch crossed his arms.

"You won't be able to join me there." Shrugging unconcernedly, I turned the steering wheel and crawled toward the exit. "Don't say I didn't warn you. Brooklyn told me why none of you can enter the reservations."

It wasn't the whole truth. She'd told me they couldn't cross the boundaries of the reservations because of the Shamans but not the logistics of it. After that, I kind of put the two and two together and didn't bother her with questions. The poor girl had too much going on for me to add more with my curiosity. Not that I could stop myself sometimes, but A for effort and all that.

Bad River Reservation sat on the south coast of Lake Superior with a population of only one thousand, four hundred and seventy-nine people. After I lost my mom, I never spoke about her much, not even to Brooklyn whom I considered a very close friend. She moved out of Bad River to be with my father, and she was the reason why I was welcomed to most tribe lands with the exception of a few that wanted nothing to do with me. The Ojibwe tribe would open their doors to me, but I had no idea if they'd be able to help my friend. I still had to ask.

"You might hunker down on the side of the road and wait until I return and pick you up," I told Rowen as we drove out of the manicured lawns through the elaborate iron gates. "You still have time to jump out and go back home to wait for the guys." My hands were already sweating around the leather of the steering wheel.

What if the Shaman said no? Or, worse, what if he said

there was nothing he could do to help Brooklyn? I know my friend thought she'd only put me in danger since that night when she showed up in my kennel. The truth was, ever since I met Brooklyn she gave me my life back, a purpose. I lost my family and apart from the animals I had nothing to give me hope for the future. I was drifting. Running for my life and monsters trying to rip me apart might not be much of a good time but for the first time after my father died I felt all the missing pieces coming together.

I felt whole.

Like this world was where I should've been the entire time.

"I will wait," Rowen grumbled under his breath while staring out the window in the darkness.

Humming my reply distractedly, I pressed on the gas. Dominic said Brooklyn was lost to blood lust. There must be some sort of cure for it. If the Shaman doesn't know it, maybe she would offer some help in finding it. I never thought I'd be calling in on favors where I'd adamantly refused any before. But this was worth reminding people of things.

Brooklyn was worth it.

She did save this Shaman's life after all.

Even if she didn't know what she was before she gave her to me.

Chapter Nine

DOMINIC

Ice cold wind ripped at my skin as I weaved through the streets of Chicago, gripping the bike with enough strength to make the metal groan under my palms. Bright, blinding lights blazed at my irises as the blaring of horns, along with the stench of hot asphalt and exhaust fumes, assaulted my senses. Samir was zig zagging through traffic ahead of me, taking the lead when we entered the city and human scum cut me off a few times by boxing me in between their shiny vehicles.

I wanted to shift and rip into them with hunger born out of desperation.

Sound and smell were unrecognizable through downtown, yet my ears pricked in hopes to hear anything that might alert me of the Syndicate assholes roaming the town. I didn't delude myself that the Council would wait long before searching for her. They were everywhere, lurking in the shadows in hopes of getting their hands on her and dragging her back to that hell on earth.

The things Samir shared with me when he spoke of the

prophecy haunted my dreams, and it wasn't me that lived through that nightmare.

Brooklyn did.

Things that would make a grown male weep and constantly look over his shoulder made the female someone I could only stare at in awe. Instead of a broken mind and cruelty, what she went through made her kind, loyal to those she trusted, and compassionate beyond belief. The tears rolling down her cheeks when I spoke of my family's death would torment me to my last breath.

I had to find her.

My bike rolled to a stop at the traffic lights next to Samir's shiny toy. The window hummed as it rolled down and my teeth clenched when I saw him stare at me from the corner of my eye. The older they were the more frustrating dealing with the Atua became. They had patience the rest of us, mostly me, lacked.

"What?" My growl brought a smile to his stupid face.

"We should split up when we reach the industrial part of town." His tone was drenched in amusement at my agitation. "I'll take one end, you take the other, and we will meet in the middle."

"Fine." Not that I had any intention of following his plan.

"The Syndicate is already spread out around the city. It'll be easy to track her tonight."

"And you know this how?" Finally turning to lock eyes with him, my nostrils flared. It was all mind-fucking-games with his kind as long as they felt like they knew something no one else did. Samir was no different.

"No amount of blood lust would override her hatred for the Syndicate. She'll be hunting them down one by one." The smile on his face grew wicked but there was no humor in it. "If we follow the bodies, they'll lead us to her."

"If you find her first, let me know." I palmed the phone sitting in the back pocket of my jeans, and I saw his nod just as the light turned green.

Then I was gone, buildings blurring all around me.

Soon, all the happy flickering ads and billboards were replaced with debilitated structures, metal cranes reaching for the sky like skeletal arms and broken windows in gray warehouses yawning in the darkness. Chain fences rattled with each wave of cold air passing through and dogs barked somewhere in the distance. The bike slowed and rolled through the empty streets as I swerved it left and right to avoid the cracks and holes in the pavement. Trash and crushed cans littered the sidewalks as newspapers flapped on the wind like wings of dying birds.

A shriek pierced the night.

My head tilted, and I held my breath to pinpoint the direction just as a roar, neither human nor animal, echoed through the buildings. I pushed the bike in an alley, leaning it on the stand and gave chase. It would've been easier if I shifted, but Brooklyn was not herself. Seeing my animal form could do damage instead of helping the situation. With my boots thudding over the pavement, I rounded a corner and skidded to a stop.

Between a car service business and a square uninhabited warehouse, four figures faced off. Three burly males, one wielding a sword and two with daggers circled a female I'd recognize anywhere. Her red hair was wild around her face and the skin-tight clothing emphasized every curve of her body. A fourth male was sprawled at her feet, his head dangling from her fingers before she flung it a few feet away from the carcass.

As much as it killed me, I stuck to the shadows as I inched closer. Brooklyn's face turned to the side and it lifted as she sniffed. I froze, worried she might attack me—or worse, bolt out of there. In the glow of the moon perched high in the sky I saw a line form between her brows, but she shook her head and faced the three Guardians again.

My heart rattled in my chest.

Her eyes were blood red, not a sign of the emerald color of her irises. The three males attacked as one, blades swinging and arms grabbing to apprehend her. They must've had orders to bring her in alive because none of their attacks were meant to kill. I kept gliding forward until I stood at her back.

Brooklyn was moving like water. Her body twisted and turned, bending and spinning like she was made of rubber. Her arm still had the open wound that was oozing blood out of it coating her forearm and the back of her hand. If this was how she fought in bloodlust, I'd be worried about facing her in combat. So far, every time we fought I'd been too busy fighting myself to pay closer attention to her, but now...

Fists clenched I waited to either jump in to help, or until the males were dead so I could try and reason with her. If that didn't work, I might have to knock her down and drag her unconscious back to the house. Meanwhile, she used their blades against them until she had a clear path to their necks.

The longer I watched the more impossible my task seemed.

One by one they all fell at her feet. Blood dripped from her chin and fingertips and with her back to me she panted for air. To an observer she would appear distracted, but I knew she was aware of me and my exact position. It was in the way her shoulders were loose and the weight of her body rested on the balls of her feet.

I cautiously stepped out of the darkness.

"Brooklyn, it's me." Holding both hands to the sides where she would see my palms if she turned, I inched forward. "Dominic."

Slowly, she spun around to face me. The color of her irises flickered but stayed red when she sniffed the air again. "What do you want, shifter?" Her voice was huskier, more primal. "My fight is not with you."

"Don't you remember who I am?" She tensed when I took another step forward. "We are…" What exactly were we? Friends? I kissed the female for fuck sake, and bloodlust or not, I didn't want to cockblock myself for the future as the human liked to say. "…allies."

"Allies?" She laughed, a low sultry sound that pebbled the skin on my arms and made my jeans tight. "You don't smell like an ally, kitty. Why is that?"

My mouth opened to argue, but all I ended up doing was grunting when my back slammed into the wall behind me and soft curves pressed on my front. The tips of her fangs grazed the thrumming vein on my neck and hot breath puffed across my flesh.

"Ally, you said?" Brooklyn purred, and my blood boiled when her wet tongue licked a track up all the way to the back of my ear.

Palming her ass, I jerked her as close as I could to me, and she chuckled, probably questioning my sanity while she was that close to my jugular. The short hairs on the back of my neck stood at attention, but I'd be damned if I could force myself to release her.

"I'll need you to come with me." Tone deep and raspy, it

was the animal talking more than the male in me. "You are hurt and need help."

"I think not." My back arched when she nuzzled behind my ear, her whisper driving me insane. "Why do you smell familiar? Like…"

The thundering of my heart in my ears prevented me from hearing what else she said. Her lips trailed down my throat to my shoulder and dumbly I offered my neck like a fool. Deep down I knew this was not Brooklyn, at least not in her right mind but my body had a mind of its own. My animal was not helping matters either. If she killed me in this dirty part of town, I'd deserve it.

She was straddling my thigh, her hips rocking back and forward as she kissed her way to my chin. Hard as a rock, I pressed her against me, grinding on her belly so she knew what she was doing to me. The coppery stench of blood that coated her was overpowered by her natural scent and that was enough for me. We'd tiptoed around each other long enough, so I cracked like an overcooked egg under her hands. When she grazed the corner of my mouth with her smiling lips, I chased her to steal a kiss, consequences be damned.

Brooklyn pulled away before I could fuse our lips together, her red gaze searching mine. Her breathing was as labored as mine, so I wasn't the only idiot in the situation we found ourselves in. It shouldn't have made me feel better, but it did.

"Why do you smell like that?" she murmured, and I nearly came undone when her hungry eyes locked on my mouth and she licked her lips.

"I smell like what?" My foolish question made her grin at me. It took effort to keep my eyes on hers.

"Like you are mine." It took a second to register what

she said, but the next thing I knew, her lips were on me and every thought fled from my mind.

With a pained groan, I flipped us around and nudged my hips between her legs. Holding her against the wall, I devoured her mouth, my skin stretching too tight to contain me when her small hands clawed at my shoulders. Her taste overwhelmed my senses, and I was a moment from tearing her clothing when I felt eyes on us. We both stiffened at the same time.

Brooklyn's eyes met mine and a hole opened in my chest at the hurt I saw there. She thought I betrayed her somehow. "Maybe not allies after all."

My hands tightened on her, but she already slipped around me and flattened me on the wall with a hard kick to my spine. Bones cracking, my face scraped against the rough surface, but by the time I turned, she was already gone. Molars grinding, I watched her lithe body move as she disappeared in the darkness.

"Why are you here?" I snarled at Samir when he stepped out of the shadows.

"I thought you were trying to catch her, not fuck her in a pissed filled alley." The Atua sneered at me.

"I was trying to catch her, just… Fuck." With a huff, I scrubbed a hand down my face. "I got carried away. She is different."

Arching an eyebrow, he cocked his head. "I see."

"You see nothing." Pissed at being distracted, I stomped toward the bike. "I'll find her again."

He scanned the bodies littering the ground as I passed him. "Let's hope you find her before the Syndicate does."

Spinning on my heel, I punched him in the face hard enough to sprawl him on the ground. "I'd stay quiet now if I were you."

Samir watched me with an unreadable expression on his face, but he didn't try to stand up. I knew my eyes were lit up from within since my animal was stretching and pushing to be released. I still had Brooklyn's taste on my tongue and it was driving me mad. Fear for her life along with the need she woke in me was an unbearable combination.

Forgetting about the bike, I turned and shifted.

With a ferocious cry, I bounded through the night.

I should've used the motorcycle because the male in me searched for the female to take her to safety. But it was too late for that.

My animal was on the prowl.

He was searching for its mate, but so was I.

Chapter Ten

ALICE

Grateful for the darkness that hid the ugly reality of the state of the reservation, I hugged myself tighter to ward off the chill. Howls split the night seemingly from everywhere and gooseflesh spread down my back. Maybe I should've tried to get Rowen in, if for nothing else, I could trip him if anything started giving chase. The thought made me snort. As weird as the dude was, he'd started growing on me.

I'd hate to see him die.

"Who goes there?" A silhouette of a man darkened the screen door of a barely standing house as if the flimsy thing would keep him safe. A few of the nailed wooden boards on the windows which hung crookedly to the side cracked with a squeak on the strong breeze to punctuate his words.

"It is I." Hand raised in a greeting, I called out.

The same moment I had to fight the urge to smack my forehead. Who even talked like that anymore. "It is I," I muttered under my breath before calling out louder to Jim. "It's me, Jim. It's Alice."

Shivers rushed through me when the wind picked up, so ducking my head lower, I sped up toward the cracked stairs where Jim was waiting for me with an unimpressed twist to his mouth. Not that it mattered to me if he liked me being here or not. He could move to a different reservation if my presence bothered him for all I cared.

"No dogs?" Jim asked with a condescending tone.

It was on the tip of my tongue to tell him that one mutt was enough in his house and he didn't need the competition, but I needed his help so I swallowed the retort and smiled thinly as I passed him.

"No. It's just me tonight." The moment the warmth from his home washed over me, my shoulders dropped and I closed my eyes in hopes to center myself. "I'm in a desperate need for help or I wouldn't be coming unannounced like this."

I figured it would be best to just come out and tell him the truth instead of trying to play games. Jim was too smart for his own good and the moment he figured out I needed a favor he would've asked for too high of a price just to spite me. Not exactly because he was a bad person but more to teach me a lesson to simply ask next time.

"And what made you think I'd be willing to help?" Closing the door behind me, he gave me a side-eye and reluctantly moved toward the kitchen.

I could've killed for a hot cup of tea.

"That's the thing." Rubbing my upper arms to quickly bring some warmth to my body, I trailed after him. "I'm not even sure that you can help, but I'm hoping you'll at least know to point me in the direction of someone who can."

He didn't answer me although I could hear the cogs turning in his head from across the room. As much as I wanted to start spitting questions, I knew the situation was very delicate and I had to tread carefully for all our sakes. Yet again I was rethinking the wisdom of leaving Rowen on the side of the road, this time for different reasons. Maybe threatening Jim with magic would be a better tactic than asking nicely.

"Tea?"

It wasn't a question so I didn't answer him, but I did plop my butt on one of the wooden chairs. The stale scent of tobacco and alcohol lingered in the space along with the smell of pizza. The empty boxes piled up in the corner of the kitchen would've spoken about Jim's diet without the heavy pepperoni stench stabbing my nostrils—not that I would've told him that. If Dominic or Brooklyn were here, their reaction would've spoken volumes since they'd been gagging by now.

The thought of my friends cleared out any nausea starting to crawl up my throat.

"What brings you here, Alice, in the middle of the night?"

My heart picked up speed at the tiredly spoken question. "My closest friend is in trouble and I have to find a way to help her."

Jim, much to his displeasure, was appointed as a person I could contact twenty-four-seven when I have a drop off for the reservation. Not a big fan of outsiders, the poor man still managed to tolerate me and my quirks like a champ. Tonight might change our dynamic forever, but I was willing to burn a bridge to save Brooklyn.

"Coming all the way here for boy problems in the middle of the night was not a very smart idea, girl."

"She's not human." Jaw rigid, I fisted my hand for

blurting it out. A deaf man could hear my accelerated breathing, but apart from the stiffening of his shoulders, Jim showed no other reaction to my poorly planned outburst.

"Not human, huh?" Snatching a cup from the pile next to the sink, he wiped the inside with his shirt. Lifting it at the eye level he checked it for a second and with a shrug he filled it with the steaming tea.

I would've lost my mind about the germs and whatnot if I wasn't desperate for his help.

"Yeah." A sigh whooshed out of me. "Not a Skinwalker." I mumbled while watching for a reaction through my lashes.

"I see." Tea made, he plopped the cup with a loud thump in front of me and chose to stay across the room by leaning back on the sink.

"She saved my life more times than I can count." Holding his narrowed gaze steadily I waited for emphasis. "I'm not leaving without at least an idea of who knows how to help her. I've done a lot for your shaman, it's his turn now."

"Have you now?" A muscle ticked in his jaw, but of course I ignored it. What was he going to do? Kill me? "I believed that was an altruistic act on your part, young lady. I should've known it was hiding a Machiavellian nature."

"Seriously, Jim?" Fighting the urge to throw the cup of hot tea at his head, I glared at him. The damn glasses slid down my nose, so I shoved them back hard enough to bring tears to my eyes when the plastic hit a bone. "We are starting with insults now?"

His mouth opened, but I had no more time left for messing around. Pushing off the chair, I rounded the small island and got in his face. Well, technically with his chest since he was much taller than me not that it stopped my attitude.

"They poisoned her with tainted blood and now she's crazy with bloodlust and doesn't remember who she is." Stiffening my forefinger, I poked between his newly formed man boobs as hard as I could. "I need her to remember, Jim, and you are going to help me find a cure."

Blood rushed between my ears creating white noise and it drove me insane. The fear raked my insides. Everything I suppressed so I could think rationally and didn't get crippled by it returned with vengeance, buckling my knees. For that reason, I missed the blanching of Jim's face, or the fact he was gripping my upper arms to a point of bruising.

"Tonight." I told him. "You'll help me find help for her tonight."

"Jumlin." The raw rasp coming from him sounded nothing like Jim.

I took a step back.

Swallowing thickly, he grabbed the sink to hold himself up and gaped at me with horror filled eyes. "You want to help a Jumlin." Fear stabbed through me because he was paling more by the second.

"I want you to help my friend." Speaking slowly—like to a child—I gingerly reached for him in case he dropped. "I have no idea what a Jumlin is, but she's not it. Promise. She's an Atua."

With everything in me I hoped I was telling him the truth. I mean, whatever word he used wasn't even close to Atua, which Brooklyn claimed she was. Stuck in my head, I missed what Jim muttered under his breath.

"What?" My eyebrows tugged on my forehead as I focused on his face again.

"A monster," Jim hissed. "You want me to save a vampire."

Well, crappity crap cakes.

Maybe he knew what she was better than Brooklyn did herself. To my dismay, I snorted out loud at the absurdity of the situation.

Chapter Eleven

DOMINIC

I believed myself to know and understand anguish.

After all, I lost my whole family at the hands of the Syndicate and spent longer than an average human life blaming myself for their deaths. If I'm not mistaken someone called it a survivor's guilt, too.

Brooklyn's scent tantalized my soul, barely penetrating my sense of smell before dissipating and it yanked me out of my thoughts.

I was playing a dangerous game by allowing myself to daydream during a hunt. Because no matter if I liked it or not it was a hunt. One that would not end in death if I'm lucky.

Samir's presence was like a dull ache in the back of my skull, one that my animal easily ignored. He kept pace with me, not surprising given his nature, but not an easy task to be sure. As much as I wanted to do this alone and my hackles were up just from thinking about him being around my mate, I had to rein in my instincts for her sake. With tremendous effort, I shifted back to my human form.

"We need to talk." Not breaking a stride, I spoke soft enough that only a supernatural could hear it.

"If I didn't see you humping Brooklyn's leg like a horny rabbit a minute ago I would've been happy to oblige." Materializing smilingly from out of nowhere, the blood-sucker pointedly looked down at my erection.

Reluctantly, I looked at it too.

It bobbed with each step I took, pointing ahead of me like an arrow. A very red and angry looking arrow if I was to be honest with myself. It annoyed me more than Samir's comment. I knew it was said in jest, but I couldn't help myself.

"Feel free to bow down and kiss it, leech." I even pointed at it by swirling my hand with flourish.

"Tempting."

Snorting at his wistful tone, I rolled my shoulders to relieve the tension that was clamping my muscles and the back of my skull in a vise. "We need a plan."

"Now he wants to talk about a plan." His hand came up between us to stop me from telling him to fuck off. "Okay, let us not argue, that was very childish of me. What do you suggest?"

Sirens blared from somewhere deeper in the city, breaking the silence in the industrial part where the asphalt itself seemed to be holding its breath for something. Although I couldn't sense anyone, I checked our surroundings by glancing from side to side, noting the boarded windows and cut wire on the chain-link fences. A few raindrops splattered on my forehead and nose so I lifted my face toward the sky hoping to see less clouds than what was hanging overhead.

"To be realistic, I can't bring myself to hurt her even for her own good. And you"—giving him a side-eye, I smirked at his glare— "you couldn't hurt her if you tried. Let's be honest here, Samir, the female is a weak spot." And to soothe his ego I added, "For both of us." A twist to my mouth let him know I was doing him a favor.

"That she is." He conceded with a reluctant nod.

"We need to trick her." Catching a whiff of Brooklyn's scent, I changed direction leading us between two nondescript buildings that had seen better days.

"Are we talking about the same female?" Samir muttered, not questioning my tracking skills. "Last time I checked she outsmarted all of us and wreaked havoc over all of Chicago."

"Yes, we are. But unless you have a better idea on how to help her without causing her harm, we need to be smarter."

A soft scrape over the pavement to my left made me pause. Pressing my palm to the center of Samir's chest, I stopped him, too, although I didn't have to do it. His head was cocked to the side, telling me he also heard the noise.

The night was turning pretty gloomy, the moonlight unable to penetrate the thick clouds to aid us. Straining my eyes, I employed all my senses to better judge what was coming our way when a screech was followed by a small dark shape darting across the street from the closest alley.

Samir choked down a laugh which I was pretty sure saved his life. If he barked it out, my fist would've punched through his chest.

"Pesky little creatures," he rasped, coughing to hide the lifting of his tone. "Cats." A snort followed it.

"I said I can't bring myself to harm Brooklyn, Samir. I never said anything about you." My glower broke through his control.

The jerk laughed.

Raising both his hands in surrender, he took a couple of steps away from me. "I meant no insult, Dominic. Little humor never hurt anyone."

"It can hurt you right now."

"But it won't." Taking a deep breath, he dropped his hands to hang limply at his sides. "What do you have in mind for our girl?"

It took me a moment to realize the terror rising growl lifting the short hairs on my nape was coming from me.

"Easy there." All humor evaporated from Samir. "She is like a daughter to me. You know this."

Logically, I did know that he felt some paternal connection to Brooklyn and to some degree a sense of duty and honor by protecting her. Try telling that to my animalistic brain that was feeding anger to my beast telling him to kill anyone who tried to stake a claim to his mate. Nostrils flaring, I bared my teeth at the male watching me warily.

"You are really pushing it, Samir." The deep color painting my words told him I was more beast than male at that moment. Lungs expanding as far as I could inflate them, I took deep breaths in hopes to calm down. "Now's a good time to start throwing ideas on how to corner my mate. I need her safe." And away from you, but I didn't tell him that.

"If you piss me off I'll tranq you, Dominic. You know as well as I do that short of knocking her out, we can't make her do anything she doesn't want to do." He told me with a slump to his shoulders. Maybe he thought he was safe? I didn't peg him for a fool but who knew. "That's it!"

Involuntarily, I hissed in his direction when he shouted that last part.

"Hear me out." Standing still even though I could tell it was difficult, Samir kept eye contact.

A blind male could see how much it took from him to not attack, so I had to give him some credit. Continuing to take deep even breaths, I locked my muscles to stay where I was. Another siren pierced the silence of this part of Chicago, spiking my heart rate for a second.

"That's just it. If we find a way to knock her out long enough for us to restrain her in some way, we can take our time in figuring out a cure." Speaking fast to get it all out before I totally lose control of my animal, Samir watched me expectantly.

It took a long moment for his words to penetrate the fog in my brain, but when they did, all anger disappeared. It was replaced with determination like I'd never felt before.

"Samir, you are a genius." It was comical to see the emotions play out on his usually stoic face.

"Can you repeat that again?" Head slightly tilted to the side, he leaned toward me.

"No." Snatching his upper arm, I marched him back in the direction where we'd left our transports. "But I'm all ears to hear about this tranquilizer that you mentioned."

The sky opened above us and rain poured out as if from a faucet. It helped keep my control over my beast as it chilled my otherwise overheated skin. Shifting always raised my core temperature for some inexplicable reason. Even my parents were perplexed by it when I was growing up.

"How would tranquilizing you help us catch Brooklyn?" He sounded genuinely confused. "Not that I would mind knocking you out, just so we are clear."

"You're not putting me to sleep so don't get any crazy ideas or you may lose your head." Pushing him ahead of me made him stumble a few steps just as his face cleared from any bewilderment he previously felt. "We will be putting Brooklyn to sleep."

"That is genius." Samir puffed up his chest.

"Wanna clue me in on your plan, boys?" Brooklyn purred from the darkness.

We both spun in her direction just in time to see her casually find her way in the open from between a warehouse to our left and some factory to our right. The way her feet glided her toward us was nothing short of a prowl.

Samir's profanities made her throw her head back and laugh. I, on the other hand, gaped at my mate like a male untried.

"Hello again, kitty cat." She winked playfully just as her scent reached me like a punch to the back of the head, leaving me dazed. I had to lock my knees before I dropped down and crawled toward her.

I was unsuccessful in resisting her. Like a fool, I lunged for my mate, but she masterfully dodged me and disappeared somewhere into the dark alleys of the city.

My scream shook the very foundations of Chicago.

Chapter Twelve

ALICE

I believed there was a good reason why Brooklyn never wanted to advertise who handed me the animals I brought to the shamans, but it never crossed my mind I'd get the reaction I was seeing on Jim.

He wasn't even a medicine man.

Deep down, like a bad omen, I had a feeling that the moment I mentioned my friend, and what she really was, inside the reservation something shifted in the very fabric of life.

Something fundamental.

There was no going back now that the truth was out, so I just had to do the best I could with what I had in front of me. It wasn't much, but that seemed to be the popular theme lately. For a brief moment, I debated telling Jim about my newfound powers, but I dismissed the idea immediately.

There were more pressing matters to deal with and he was on the verge of passing out as it was.

"If you stop hyperventilating, I'll explain." Eyeing Jim

while he was inching away from me, my brain whirled with ideas on how to prevent him from bolting out the door. Stupid, really, since this was his house and not mine.

With a huff, I jabbed my glasses up my nose where they kept sliding down and glared at the man. "Honestly, Jim, you're making this out to be a bigger deal than it actually is."

"You've been brainwashed, girl." He spat the accusation at me, and it took everything I had not to slap him. "Get out of here before you get us all killed."

"I want nothing more than to get out of here." If Dominic found out I was not in the house, he would lock me up until I was old and wrinkled.

"So here is an idea." Pretending that I was very excited, I clapped my hands with each word. "You tell me how to help my friend and I'll be gone from your life forever. Deal?" Blinking with enthusiasm, I waited.

"They have messed with your mind." Jim nodded slowly to himself, making me scowl at him. "You are crazy." Without looking, he reached back on the makeshift kitchen counter and grabbed a half empty bottle of some type of whisky.

"That's actually rude to say to people in today's society." I snatched the bottle from his hand when he tried his best to guzzle whatever was left inside it.

Whisky sprayed over both of us, trickling down Jim's face into his shirt. The stench from the alcohol immediately mixed with the tobacco and pepperoni one coming out of the furniture and rugs, so I had to focus very hard not to start gagging.

"What do you want, demon?" Some pathetic expression of defeat fell over his features. "What can I offer you to leave my soul in one piece?"

"Seriously?" When he just kept staring at me, I did what any normal woman would do when faced with the same predicament.

I slapped him.

Like, really hard.

"Let's try this again, Jim." The look of shock he gave me would've been comical, but I was running out of time and patience. Plus, his reaction was freaking me out to no end. "I need to help my friend. Do you know how?"

I spent a few minutes explaining to him what happened to Brooklyn without giving too much details. The poor schmuck was freaked out as it was without mentioning shifters and witches on top of everything. "If not, tell me who knows how to help her, so I can get out of your hair and you can keep your soul." If he heard the sarcasm in that last part, he didn't show it.

"Laughing Crow is the only one that knows if such a thing exists," he finally muttered under his breath and I had to strain to hear him.

"Is she home?" Mentally I was already calculating the time it would take me to get to her house.

She lived on the edge of the reservation which luckily was not one of the larger ones we had.

"She should be." Suddenly the cloudiness cleared from Jim's eyes and he pinned me with his gaze. "Be careful, girl. If anything happens to Laughing Crow, you'll have every shaman gunning for your head."

"I need her help, why would I hurt her? Have you met me?" Flapping my hand in front of his face until he slapped it away, I shook my head in disappointment. "It's me. Alice. The same Alice that helps all of you with anything you need."

"When you play with monsters you will become one

yourself." Regaining some of his sanity, Jim looked around his small kitchen with freakish intensity, searching for the universe knew what.

"How very enlightening." Leaving him to his craziness, I headed for the door.

Hoping that the reservation shaman would be little less of a fruit loop, I waved at the still pale man gaping at my departure and closed the screen door with more force than was necessary to convey my great displeasure with his behavior.

And promptly screamed from the top of my lungs when I came face to face with Rowen.

"Silence," he hissed, and slapping a hand over my mouth, twisted left and right to see if anyone came out to investigate.

My eyes felt too big for my face, and my heart was trying its best to punch through my rib cage. Panting for breath behind Rowen's palm, I clung to his forearm so I didn't drop at his feet. My legs were kinda shaky, I'm not gonna lie.

He scared the bejesus out of me.

"Are you trying to get us killed?" Robe dude had the decency to glower at me accusingly. You'd think I asked him to get in my face the second I exited the house.

"No." I huffed, sucking in deep breaths in hopes to calm down. All my insides were shaky thanks to the witch and his damn ninja skills. "How about you?"

The door behind us opened, and with just one quick look at me and Rowen, Jim slammed it closed again in our faces.

"No luck with the cure, judging by the look on your face." I must've shown my confusion because his chin tipped at the closed door. "A friend of yours, I presume." Rowen grinned at my scowl like a fool. "He seems as pleasant as you. Like a porcupine."

"Just so you know, I will find a way to help Brooklyn." Shouldering my way past him, I had every intention to stomp away from the witch. "Where is my wolf?"

"I left him to wait in the vehicle." Rowen attempted to follow me.

My feet had a mind of their own, however, and I tripped over clean, flat ground. With a shriek, I started going down, face first. Rowen took hold of a fistful of my shirt and yanked me back before I could embarrass myself and faceplant.

Not breaking a stride, I kept talking like nothing happened while pushing my glasses back up my nose. "Good, because I can't deal with both of you at the same time. And when Brooklyn's back to herself I'll tell her that you've been mocking me and almost scared me to death. She'll suck you dry like a juice box."

An unimpressed grunt was my answer.

"Did anyone tell you she's not a big fan of witches as it is?" Glancing over my shoulder, I smiled wide at his narrowed gaze.

"Thank you, Rowen, for preventing my fall." His eyebrows crawled up his forehead as he muttered mockingly, "Don't mention it, human. It was a pleasure."

"It's your fault I almost fell, dude." All these supernaturals were unbelievably confusing. "How did you get here, anyway? You shouldn't be able to cross into any of the reservations."

"It appears that witches are welcomed as long as there is no intent to harm." He was extremely proud of himself with that discovery, judging by the way his smile brightened up his face.

"Oh goody. Let's not share that info with anyone. Okay?"

"Why do I sense mockery in your tone?"

"Because I learned that skill from the best, oh master."

Snorting at my antics and shaking his head, he joined me on the dirt road toward the other end of the reservation. If the shaman didn't want to help me, maybe the witch could zap her and change her mind. At least he would be useful for something. I gave him a side-eyed once over.

"I don't like the way you are looking at me," Rowen mumbled, his movements stiffening up immediately.

My smile stretched wider at seeing his discomfort. Maybe Dominic was rubbing off on me.

Not that I'd admit that to cat man.

Chapter Thirteen

DOMINIC

"The human is careless with her life." Samir scowled at the piece of paper he found magically pinned to the door of his bedroom. Courtesy of Rowen, no doubt.

Just like him, I wanted to find the little prick and skin him alive, but I had to think rationally if I was to be good for anyone. The situation was getting worse and worse by the minute. Running around on pure instinct proved to be as dumb as one would imagine.

My feet were making squelching sounds on the tiles with each step I took.

"This is a good thing. She's inside shaman territory." Waving away his concern, I proceeded toward the kitchen, the squeaky sound of my boots on the tiles as background music. All that shifting downtown had made me ravenous, making it difficult to think coherently. I could eat an elephant. "Brooklyn will be happy to know her friend is safe."

"And what did the witch think to do?" Trailing behind

me, Samir still clutched the letter in a tight fist. The crinkling of the paper was a nail to my brain. "Stand sentinel in front of a reservation?"

"Do you mind?" I growled at him through clenched teeth, pointedly staring at his hand until he dropped the damn thing unceremoniously to the ground. "And, do you really care that much, for that matter?"

"Not particularly, no." A careless shrug was an answer to my knowing smirk when I locked gazes with him.

Samir cared about the witch because it was a useful tool that could be manipulated to his whim. Nothing more and nothing less. Another unapologetic shrug by the ancient male followed when I was done rampaging through the whole kitchen with no luck in finding food. After I slammed the cabinet door with a loud smack out of frustration, my stomach growled like an angry bear which only amused the bloodsucker more.

"I can wait until you hunt something down to fill your belly," Samir offered, indicating the pitch-black back yard visible to supernatural sight through the floor to ceiling windows. The grin he was fighting made his words sound choked up. "Go. I'll start thinking about what we can use to apprehend Brooklyn and put her to sleep. I don't need you staring at me while I'm doing it."

Dizziness made the kitchen spin for a moment and I leaned forward to clutch the granite like it was the only thing keeping me grounded to this life. Cold sweat trickled down my spine and numbness spread through my limbs nearly pushing me down on my knees. Tongue too thick for my mouth, I breathed deeply until the spell passed and was eternally grateful Samir made no remarks or jokes about the state I was in. It took a long second for my heartbeat to return to the regular rhythm while I panted harshly, my forehead pressed to the cool kitchen countertop.

"You don't need to feed?" I ground out through my teeth in hopes of keeping some semblance of control. What a conversation had with normality was beyond me but there was no rhyme or reason to anything today.

My distorted reflection on the stainless-steel fridge squinted back at me.

"Not for another week or so." Poised to catch me if I tipped over, the male watched me with a closed off expression. For a second there, I wondered if he expected me to shift and attack him but dismissed it immediately. On my side or not, Samir was a member of the Council. If he even suspected that there was a possibility I would indeed attack, he would've been attached to my jugular like the leech he was before I had time to blink.

"It must be nice." A pathetic snort was all I could muster for his sake. It did ease the stiffness to his shoulders, however, so I called it a win.

Samir's humorless grin in answer was not a pleasant sight. Lost in my own frustration and impotence to help the female that took over my life like a storm, I kept forgetting that he cared about her, too. As much as he disliked admitting any vulnerability, it wasn't hard to notice the strained lines bracketing his mouth or the corners of his eyes. Samir and I worked together out of necessity all these years until Brooklyn decided my life was worth saving that night.

Now...

Now we had more in common apart from a goal to screw the Syndicate every way we could. Both of us had her. Logically, I knew we would do anything to protect her. Well, I would do anything and he better make sure he did.

Otherwise, I had no qualms about ending him. With that in mind, I pushed off of the granite, and with a determined stride, headed out.

Rain was steadily pelting down on me when I stepped on the back patio, drowning the sound of the door sliding back into place. Riding the bike made sure I was already soaked to the bone so it made no difference. It only added to my annoyance that it hadn't stopped. I'd never admit it to Brooklyn, but I hated the rain. She might think of me as unworthy, which made my animal so destressed it felt like it was rattling my bones.

Following that thought, sharp pain stabbed me in the center of the chest almost doubling me over. I had to find a way to save my mate. Her taste was still strong on my tongue and urgency was clawing my insides driving me insane. Failure was unacceptable.

Not now when I just found her.

Maybe this was my punishment for refusing to acknowledge what my beast knew from day one. A penance for thinking she was the enemy instead of the precious thing she really was.

A mate.

If I'd learned anything in the years after my family's death it was that dwelling on the past never helped solve anything. I had to keep myself busy and focused if I was to help my female. First, I needed food. Then, a plan.

Lifting my face up and closing my eyes, I inhaled deeply. Many scents mingled around the mansion but the game was hard to hide from me. The musky smell of wet soil and crushed grass under many paws teased my senses to give chase. They hoped to survive the night but were aware they were my prey. My beast rose close to the surface and even their heartbeats drummed a beat in my ears.

I wondered if this was how my mate heard my heart-beat, too. A fluttering drumbeat against my rib cage whenever she was near.

That thought pushed me to shift and I gave chase.

The sooner the hunt was over, the faster I could go bring my mate home.

Chapter Fourteen

ALICE

Okay, so maybe the decision about coming to see a shaman in the middle of the night without Dominic or Brooklyn as a backup was a dumb idea. See? I was not too proud to admit it when I was wrong.

Admit it in my head, that was.

Like hell I would say that out loud in front of holier than thou supernatural beings. No, thank you. They had enough arrogance without it. Believe you me.

Rowen had started to rise from his crouch to better see what the hullabaloo in front of the barely standing house was when I yanked him back down by jerking on his robes. With a shocked gasp, he dropped on his back like a turtle and proceeded to glare at me after he caught his breath.

I ignored him, of course.

A metal container came sailing through the air from the side of the house we were observing. It resembled a tiny UFO blinking at us under the yellow glow of the street lamp which was tilting precariously over the fenced yard across from our hiding spot. With a sharp smack, the container slammed loudly on the trunk of a sad looking tree before slapping in a large puddle formed on the dirt road by the steady drizzle which had started not long ago.

Because why not, right?

If she made the weather colder than a witches' tit that night so I could freeze my ass off, might as well Mother Nature could give me an involuntary shower, too.

A wooden bowl was hurled next.

The weight of the material prevented it from visiting our side of the road, fortunately. According to how things progressed so far, I had no doubt it would've smacked me in the head if it reached me. The propelling of the object was followed by a string of expletives that made the tips of my ears warm up. I couldn't see them but had no doubt they were a nice shade of lobster red.

I also made sure to avoid eye contact with Rowen.

Robe dude was not unaffected either by the aforementioned sacrilegious description of appendages being shoved in places they had no business entering, so he awkwardly cleared his throat a few times before realizing we needed to stay quiet. I was mentally ready to come face to face with a shaman but we had no clue what was going on in her house. Or her basement to be exact. By the look of things, she was doing a crazy version of pissed off spring cleaning.

"Stay here until I call you to come out." Craning my neck to peek over the foliage in case something else was chucked our way, I mumbled under my breath to Rowen without looking at him.

My knees were digging deeper in the mud as I stretched to see better, but I looked a mess anyway, plus the pants were not mine, they belonged to the arrogant vampire with a perky butt. Not like I was looking at his butt per se, or trying to win any beauty pageants for that matter. I was totally not into perky butts or monk wanna-be dudes in robes either. If I wanted to look like a three-hundred-year-old swamp hag out for the night, it was my right to rock the look.

"I think I'm going to take my chances and go see what's going on. We don't have all night to sit here getting drenched." Decision made, I was ready to march across the street and get it over and done with.

When no reply came, I glanced at robe dude with a smartass remark on the tip of my tongue just to irk him so I could repel the image stuck in my head of Samir's flexing buttocks.

Promptly my spine snapped ramrod straight when my gaze locked with his pale glass-like irises. The Rowen I knew was nowhere to be found. It looked like he was in a trance but that was not what made the short hairs on the back of my neck rise. A faint glow emanated from deep within his eyes that stole my breath away. Thankfully for both our sakes, I was wrenched out of the daze by a haunted howl from a wolf somewhere in the distance. In the few seconds it took to get lost in the glow of his gaze, I crawled toward him and was almost in his lap, the tip of my nose nearly touching his.

Totally invading his personal space.

Another howl, this one much closer than the first, made me jerk back from him so hard I landed on my ass and crab-walked away as fast as the slippery mud would allow me.

"Why are you here?" Rowen's lips were moving but sure as hell that was not his voice. Unless he had the ability to switch his gender because that was one hundred percent a woman speaking through him.

My nose tickled from a raindrop that was sliding painfully slow around the rim of my glasses, but I was too busy hyperventilating to concentrate enough and scratch it. That was until the third howl pierced the night. It scared me enough to jump off the ground and snap out of whatever stupidity overtook my senses. I was not a helpless little human anymore.

Although the magic I was capable of doing came randomly and tried to hurt everyone I cared about, I still had something.

Anger bubbled in my belly, and I glared at whoever was looking through Rowen's eyes.

"Who are you?" Proud of my bravado and the fact my voice was not as shaky as my insides, I squared my shoulders. "What do you want?"

"It is you who is lurking around my territory, girl." Rowen's head cocked to the side in a birdlike manner. "Did you bring me an offering?" Tone filled with anticipation, he rocked gently back and forward.

If I'd believed I'd seen all the weird surrounding my supernatural friends in our adventures hiding from the Syndicate, I changed my mind.

This shit was a whole new level of messed up.

Acting on instinct, I took a stab in the dark. "Laughing Crow?" I mean, who else could it be at this point. The fact that the shaman could possess Rowen like some creepy ghost was freaky as hell.

I never signed up for this level of crazy.

A shrill shriek-laugh burst out of the witch, echoing down the empty road until it felt like nails on a chalkboard.

It cut off abruptly. "Did you bring an offering?" Rowen got in my face, all sense of humor erased from his features.

"I have an offering like nothing you've ever been given before, but you have to help me first," I rushed to assure her, thinking fast on my feet. Since I was down the rabbit hole anyway, I might as well check where it would lead me. "It was impossible for me to carry it here on my own. I'd have to take you to it."

The shaman narrowed Rowen's eyes to slits, leaning back to better show her displeasure and that she didn't believe a word I said. Not that I could blame her. We both knew I was lying out of my ass even if my heart wasn't thumping so hard Jim could hear it at his house through the flimsy front door he'd ceremoniously slammed in my face. The wind picked up at that moment and whistled between the trees loud enough to make me jerk like a frightened rabbit.

"You cannot take without giving," she told me somewhat distractedly. "The Great Spirit won't be willing to lend a hand otherwise. What is used needs to be replenished. It's how Mother Nature works." Rowen shrugged awkwardly. "I'm not strong enough alone to twist the energies to do my bidding."

"I can help you," I offered dumbly before I had a chance to think it through. All of us agreed it wasn't smart to share the knowledge of my newfound powers, yet here I was, discussing it like it was an everyday thing.

A thrill raced through me just thinking about it.

Powers. Me. Alice. I had powers.

"Can you now?" The glow in Rowen's eyes focused on me with an intensity that stole my breath away.

Well, it was now or never, I decided. Everything in me agreed with that because my whole demeanor changed. My spine straightened, my shoulders squared, and warmth spread through my extremities.

"Yes." I looked squarely at the creep riding Rowen's body like a beat-up Toyota purchased from a corny salesman.

"Yes, I can," I reiterated. "I have magic."

Chapter Fifteen

ALICE

A mouthful of dirt was never in the plans in my efforts to help Brooklyn, yet, here we were.

Go figure.

My belly flattened on the muddy road when a thick wooden handle, thankfully lacking the metal part of whatever tool it used to be, came sailing through the air like a projectile at my head. I ducked as fast as I could, diving for the murky puddles created by the rain like a desperate athlete gunning for gold.

Telling the shaman I had magic worked.

It worked just like... well, magic.

Laughing Crow amicably agreed for a tête-à-tête with me in her basement, which she ostensibly referred to as her catacomb, after I gave her a Reader's Digest version of Brooklyn's predicament. I realized why the second I stood at the opened doorway of the said underground level. Furthermore, it explained why she wanted me to meet her there, instead of coming to speak with me at the trees Rowen and

I used as cover for our stakeout. What, with my mentioning of magic and all that.

Potent energy buzzed through the soles of my borrowed shoes all the way to the top of my head where it tickled the inside of my skull.

A handful of mud oozed down my fingers and splattered with a squishy plop next to my foot, courtesy of the dodgeball game with the wooden handle, but I stood there gaping like a fool at the chaos. Bundles of herbs hung everywhere from the ceiling, held together by a threadbare rope that had seen better days. It was a sea of dried bouquets of wild flowers that had performed some ritualistic mass suicide by hanging. Hysteria clawed at my insides. Laughter bubbled up my throat, but I choked it down so as not to disturb the dainty woman rampaging through large piles of bowls, garden tools, and bottles.

There were so many bottles.

One of them soared across the space in my direction, forcing me to hug the side of the open door and cling to it like a drowning man would cling to a straw. She kept chucking objects without looking, and the last thing I needed were stitches on my forehead. If that meant getting frisky with the doorframe, so be it. Rowen would need to thank me many times for letting him stay behind to recover from the possession. For a witch, he sure was a scaredy cat when it came to things like that.

I kind of felt sorry for the poor guy, truth be told. I'd be traumatized too if I had to air out my butt in a robe my whole life while bloodsuckers were breathing down my neck.

"I'm here," I mumbled before clearing my throat and trying again a smidgen louder. "Laughing Crow, I'm here."

"I can smell you." She snickered before turning to look at me over her shoulder.

Nothing like I expected, she left me stunned for a second. From what I could judge, since she was bent over piles of bowls looking for something, she was shorter than me. The long-sleeved t-shirt she wore was covered in cobwebs and dust, making it difficult to determine what color it was. Her jeans didn't fare better either. A thick strand of silver in otherwise pitch-black hair obscured her right eye, but the left one was unnerving enough to send chills up and down my spine. Dark like an abyss, it had no pupil. Not one I could see at least.

"Sorry, I couldn't stop at my place and take a shower before coming to see you. I meant no offense," I drawled, annoyed to no end by her comment while resisting the urge to lift my arm and sniff my armpit. My glasses slid down my nose, so I jerked them back up with one finger none too gently, smearing dirt all over my face. Tears sprung in my eyes from it.

"Ah, but you cannot wash this scent off." Inhaling deeply, she blissfully fluttered her eyelids closed. "Magic. The Great Spirit is strong in you." A line formed between her brows at the same time my heart sped up so fast, it was literally rattling my rib cage. "As strong as it is in me." Her eyes snapped open and locked on me again. "How's that possible?"

"Do you need a hand there?" I squeaked and erratically waved a hand at the tipped over bowls behind her in hopes to distract her. The words spilled out in one breath. "I didn't mean to prevent you from finishing your task this evening." Sucking in an audible breath, I blinked owlishly at her amused face and finished lamely with, "It looks very important."

"It could be." Laughing Crow shrugged dismissively and gave me a pointed look to assure me we would return to the subject of my magic at a later date. "I was looking for... Ah ha!" With an excited shout she dove between a pile of cracked vases and a pile of dented cooking sheets on her right, emerging immediately after with a long golden feather gripped tightly in her fist.

"Okaaaay then." When the woman glowered at my fake enthusiasm I grinned brightly to salvage the damage. From where I stood, it seemed like I'd accidentally insulted her as well. "I can see why you were looking for it. It's very pretty."

It took a lot not to smack my own forehead. What on Earth was the matter with me? I needed her help for goodness's sake.

"It's for you." The shaman told me sternly, confirming my fears that I did indeed upset her. "I knew you'd come tonight but not the details of what kind of help you'd need. I should've known Jumlin, a monster, is involved when I had to come down here to find the feather." She muttered that last part under her breath with a disgusted twist to her mouth.

"About that." Forgetting all my unease and straightening my shoulders, I returned her stern expression triple fold. A pressure headache started forming between my eyebrows from how hard I was glaring at her.

Brooklyn may not have been your typical girl next door type of a being, but she was my best friend, damn it, and I wouldn't let Jim or the shaman, no matter how much I needed help, call her a monster in front of me. All she did was help everyone around her yet here they were talking bad about her and calling her names.

Between Laughing Crow, and Rowen across the street, magic was buzzing through me like I had a live wire clutched in my hand. Them insulting my friend made me feel very murder-y and no one wanted a repeat of the bread knife fiasco I had going not that long ago. There was no one around to stop me this time.

"I would stop calling Brooklyn a monster if I were you. She is my friend, and I take it personally when someone says anything but nice things about her in front of me." Speaking deliberately and clearly, I kept unblinking eye contact with the shaman whose eyes widened. A faint buzzing was coming from my hands, but I refused to glance at them. "If it weren't for her, you wouldn't have the pack of wolves that circle and protect the reservation. Or, be out of the radar for the Syndicate. So how about we learn all the facts before we name someone a monster, huh?"

"You truly care for this creature." My deepening scowl was answer enough to her slight, so she sheepishly blinked at me and cocked her head the same way she did when she'd worn Rowen like a borrowed jacket. "I do apologize for insulting your friend, Alice. I spoke hastily."

Taken aback, because I didn't expect her to apologize, I stammered a quick, "Thank you."

"When all this is over and if all of us survive what is coming, I'd very much like to meet your Brooklyn." Laughing Crow for the first time gifted me with a genuine smile. It loosened a knot in my chest that I had no idea was there. "For that to happen, however, we need to get going. We don't have much time."

Emboldened by her cordiality and hiking up my borrowed pants, that had slid down to my hips in my obstacle course adventure otherwise known as crossing the road, I inched further inside the basement.

"So, it's true then, this urge I had to come here. We can save Brooklyn." The hopeful tremor in my tone made my cheeks bloom with heat, but I couldn't care less. "You'll help me for real?"

"I can't do more than tell you how you can help your friend. What you do with the knowledge is not my concern. In two days' time, it will be the full moon." I swallowed thickly at the graveness her voice carried.

She was already turning away from me as she started talking, waving at me to follow her with one hand and wiggling the feather in the air with the other. "You'll need to summon the guardian spirits of the Air element from the East Gate to enter your circle on the night of the full moon. Your companion is a born witch, even if he is very gullible. If you've never opened a circle, he can show you how. That's why I had to find this feather. It's the last one I have from a Golden Eagle. The spirits will undoubtedly answer your call if you use it."

"Okay." I injected as much conviction as I could muster in my tone, conveying to her how seriously I took my task.

She glanced back at me and nodded approvingly.

"Here is the tricky part." Laughing Crow was turning left and right looking for something as she said this, so obviously I was staring at her, waiting to hear every word.

Because of that, I didn't see the small soup bowl in front of my foot, or the bundle of dried herbs that magically appeared in front of my face.

"Brooklyn must not resist entering the circle or this won't work so you'll need to figure that one out and outsmart her. Then, you'll need to make sure she is drained of the tainted blood as much as possible without killing her and then feed her a willing witch's blood." She stopped walking abruptly and turned to face me.

My foot landed on the edge of the small bowl, and I pitched forward so fast that a scream lodged in my throat.

My arms shot out in front of me so I could cushion my fall, but instead, I slammed both palms at the shaman's chest so hard she went flying backward wide-eyed. At the same time, a swinging bundle of the suicidal bouquets smacked me in the face and the dried stems wedged around the rims of my glasses, yanking them off my face as I went down.

I landed flat on my face with a pained, "Oomph." As the air whooshed out of me so hard I nearly fainted.

Crashing sounded all around me when Laughing Crow landed somewhere between the piles of crap she collected all her life. Not daring to move, I hoped if I played dead, she wouldn't curse me or something for being a walking disaster.

"On a second thought, maybe you should let your friend feed on you." The shaman grunted painfully. "If she kills you, she'd be doing the world a favor. You are a walking hazard, girl."

Slowly lifting my face, I found her staring daggers at me from a few feet away. "I'm not this clumsy, usually. I swear, I'm not." My rasp forced a coughing fit where I inhaled a lot of dust and who knew what kind of bacteria from the floor.

"Here." She sprang on her feet like a gazelle instead of a middle-aged woman I accidentally attacked, and snatched one of the damn bundles swaying like cobras above our heads. "Use these herbs to cleanse the space for the circle, they'll work even if it's outside. Make sure you start this exactly at midnight, it's vital that you do it right on time."

"Got it." I huffed as I lifted myself on my knees. "Start at midnight on the dot."

"Now get out of here before I change my mind and decide to keep you locked in my catacomb."

Her tone was off and my head jerked up so I could see

her. Unfortunately, my glasses were gone so she was simply a blurry blob. Blurry or not, I refused to look away from her while petting the ground blindly in search of my glasses. My fingers brushed the handle luckily, and I hastily shoved them back on just in time to see an eerie glow blooming in her irises. It reminded me of the glow in Rowen's eyes when she possessed him and my heart stopped for a long moment. That second everything became so clear that it was like a bucket of ice water being dumped over my head.

Brooklyn had me and Dominic to help her when she needed it. Who did a shaman have to ask for help if she was expecting me? Another shaman? The Great Spirit she was referring to?

I didn't stick around to ask questions or to find out. With a mumbled thank you, I took the feather and the bundle of herbs and bolted out of that basement like my ass was on fire. The shrill shriek-laugh that followed my exit formed goosebumps over my arms.

"Rowen, run!" I shouted, as I reached the road.

He didn't need to be told twice.

Chapter Sixteen

DOMINIC

I never achieved the clarity I expected from the hunt. The gnawing hunger was gone, which I guessed allowed me to rationalize better but not by much. My animal was as agitated as I was from the helplessness spreading inside me with the inability to help and protect our mate. Not that Brooklyn needed protecting. As far as I knew, she was the deadliest predator out there. Not because of her bloodline, but mostly because of the bloodlust she suffered.

There was nothing humane left in her.

With that thought, memories from earlier that night assaulted my brain and I had to stop walking or I would've ended up on my knees. The taste of her tongue gliding over mine made the blood in my veins to pump harder and faster. Closing my eyes, I lifted my face up, inhaling deeply in hopes to scent her.

"You don't smell like an ally, kitty. Why is that?"

My mouth opened to argue, but all I ended up doing was grunting when my back slammed into the wall behind me and soft curves pressed on my front. The tips of her fangs grazed the thrumming vein on my neck and hot breath puffed across my flesh.

"Ally, you said?" Brooklyn purred, and my blood boiled when her wet tongue licked a track up all the way to the back of my ear.

Palming her ass, I jerked her as close as I could to me, and she chuckled, probably questioning my sanity while she was that close to my jugular. The short hairs on the back of my neck stood at attention, but I'd be damned if I could force myself to release her.

"I'll need you to come with me." Tone deep and raspy it was the animal talking more than the male in me. "You are hurt and need help."

"I think not." My back arched when she nuzzled behind my ear, her whisper driving me insane. "Why do you smell familiar? Like..."

Her scent intensified as well as her taste in my mouth making me hard as a rock. Although I was aware that my mind was playing tricks, it did nothing to help my painful erection. Powerless to prevent it, I couldn't stop thinking about her. Not that I wanted to stop, either.

"Why do you smell like that?" she murmured, and I nearly came undone when her hungry eyes locked on my mouth and she licked her lips.

"I smell like what?" My foolish question made her grin at me. It took effort to keep my eyes on hers.

"Like you are mine." It took a second to register what she said, but the next thing I knew her lips were on me and every thought fled from my mind.

But Brooklyn was not in my arms at that moment and her nearness couldn't prevent the crippling pain crushing my chest. Sharing my painful past with her made it somewhat bearable, or so I thought. She'd made me believe that I was young when the Council killed my parents and I couldn't do anything to prevent their deaths.

What would my excuse be now when my mate's life was at stake?

My face was already tilted up, so when the roar of rage burst from me I screamed it at the cloudless sky. I was male enough to admit that it was fueled more by fear than anything else. Could I even survive enough to avenge her death if she didn't make it?

With another scream, I fell to my knees and started pounding the ground hard enough to bury my arm all the way to my elbow. Samir's presence brushed against my senses, the bloodsucker wise enough to stay out of reach. It gave me some grim sort of satisfaction that I was destroying his immaculate lawn. Petty, I know, but I could tear him limb from limb if he got within arm's reach instead of pummeling his back yard.

It was partly his fault Brooklyn was in danger.

"What's he doing? Is he planning on planting a tree or something?" Alice's voice cut off the rage so fast it made my head spin. "Oh, hey, Dominic. Fancy seeing you here." The human grinned at me, but it didn't reach her eyes.

She had information to share, but I couldn't guess if it was good or bad.

"Is that a dried weed hanging from your glasses?" Samir reached one finger out to touch the stem sticking out from her hair.

She slapped his hand away.

"Did you learn something useful, human?" The words were a rasp I forced while holding my breath. Hope never did anyone good, yet I couldn't help it. Everything in me stood suspended waiting on her answer.

I was desperate.

"I know how to bring her back to us…" Alice squeaked and hid behind Rowen when I jumped to my feet. "I'm not finished, Dominic. Don't you dare snatch me to carry me off like a sack of potatoes, cat man, I swear I'm not going to tell you anything."

Samir started laughing but coughed and covered it up when I glared at him. It seemed that redecorating his lawn didn't upset the Atua. I'd keep in mind to cover the expense for fixing it up.

"Speak," I told Alice, and she blinked at me like she didn't expect it.

"Right." Stepping out from behind the pale witch, she squared her shoulders and pushed her glasses up. "I went to one of the reservations, and no I'm not telling you which one so don't bother asking. Anywhoooo, the shaman told me how to cure Brooklyn from the bloodlust, but we can't force her inside the circle. If she resists, everything else will fail."

All four of us stood in silence.

They didn't need to share their thoughts for me to know they were thinking the same thing. How did we convince my mate to come with us and seek help willingly?

"We can use you as bait." I finally told the human. "Brooklyn will not harm you... I think."

"You think?" she screeched at me. "You think she won't hurt me, but you're not sure, huh?" My mouth opened to answer her, but she kept going. "And what if she does? Who will save her if I'm dead?"

"Rowen." With a frown, I ducked my head to look into her eyes better. She was such a tiny little creature. "He is the one born a witch. If you die, he can cure Brooklyn, can he not? Why are you asking that question? Did you hit your head?"

"Oh my god. I'm seriously debating on telling Brooklyn all this when she is back to herself. So she can be upset with you." Folding her arms over her chest, she glowered up at me. "I regret helping you kiss her. You're such a jerk."

"She didn't harm him, human." Samir rushed to calm the situation. "We found her briefly and she was close to his neck but didn't harm him. I think he was giving you a compliment by saying he thinks she won't harm you either. She cares about you as much as she cares about him."

Again, my mouth opened to correct him but whatever I was going to say died on my tongue. Alice relaxed, her arms dropping limply at her sides, and she sniffed loudly. Maybe I could've phrased it better, I'd give the Atua that much. It was never my intention to hurt the human's feelings. I was worried about my mate.

"He could've just said that," she cried out and threw herself at me, jabbing the thick frame of her glasses under my rib. "I swear you guys act like cavemen most of the time. I'll have to teach you how to use your words, cat man. It'll help you with Brooklyn, too," she told my sternum, petting my chest and promptly using my t-shirt to wipe her tears.

I gaped at her.

Samir choked.

"Do laugh," I told the Atua, lifting my furious gaze to lock on his. "I have an urge to kill something. Make it easy for me."

"I think he is using sarcasm." Rowen shuffled closer, eying me warily and whispered to Samir, you'd think he hoped I couldn't hear them. "It does not end well if you do what he says."

"You know he has like super hearing," Alice reminded the witch, and I watched his face darken with shame.

"I think I found the solution on how Brooklyn can enter the circle willingly." Samir thankfully focused on what was important. "Did the shaman mention if she has to walk into the circle on her own feet?" He squinted prudently at Alice.

"Ummm, no? The shaman didn't mention anything apart from willingly entering it," she answered and with no second thought leaned her head on my arm. I stood frozen, not knowing what to do. At the end, I petted the top of her head awkwardly. She slapped my hand away the same way she did to Samir. "I'm not your pet, Dominic. That's what we do to dogs, not friends."

"Unless that was specifically mentioned, I have found it could be used as a loophole in magic circles." Samir nodded thoughtfully, saving me from further angering the human. "Dominic and I discussed tranquilizing her, and I believe I have the answer. Let us go inside so I can share my thoughts with all of you."

With no argument from anyone, we all piled in after the male through the glass doors into the kitchen. Alice and Rowen took one tall chair each with me propping a hip on the island and crossing my arms over my chest. It took everything I had to hold myself together. Adrenalin was already pumping through my veins.

Samir walked across to the sink and leaned back on it as he locked eyes on each one of us deliberately before speaking. "I believe if we use a mercury filled tranquilizer, the element will buy us enough time to approach Brooklyn unharmed and confine her in a container of liquid nitrogen to keep her frozen until we can place her inside the magic circle."

"Day after tomorrow," Alice blurted out, raising her hand in the air. "That's when we must do this. On the night of the full moon starting exactly at midnight." The wolf who followed her like a silent shadow from the yard whined at her feet.

"I'm not sure how I feel about locking her up in a container." Shifting uneasily on my feet, I glared at the floor. "Brooklyn deserves more than that. She was caged like an animal to save our lives. I'm not going to put her through that again. Plus, let's not forget we need to lure her to meet us first for any of this to work."

"We can use the human as bait." Samir suggested low enough like he was talking to himself. "I think you were on to something earlier. If the human and I go, Brooklyn will intercept us. She won't show herself if you are there, Dominic."

"I will not let you lock her up, Samir. I'll kill you first." My beast was clear in my tone. It was the animal not the male in me talking. I'd kill them all if they tried to lock up my mate.

"Hold on, I think I have an idea," the human muttered, staring intently at Samir. "You said she needs to be enclosed in something with liquid nitrogen, correct?"

"That is what I suggest. Yes."

"What are you thinking, human?" I asked despite myself. The glint in Alice's eyes did not sit well with me.

"All you, growly man. You can figure out the bait and the tranquilizing part. I got the confinement covered." Alice was bouncing on the chair with excitement. "And don't worry cat man, our girl will not be caged, I promise. Trust me."

"Males." Samir straightened, looking affronted, you'd think the human insulted his mother by calling her a wench. "We are males, not men. We are not human."

"You say potato, I say potahto." She stuck her tongue out at him like a child.

I ignored them because my very being recoiled from the idea of trusting anyone with my mate's life, but I reminded myself that everyone in that room cared about Brooklyn. Including Rowen. Including Samir, as much as it rubbed me wrong that the Syndicate prick was still breathing.

"Do not make me regret this, Alice." I sounded raw.

Fuck, I'd never felt more raw.

"Never, Dominic." Chills spread through me when all humor vanished from her face and she faced me with seriousness and gravity in her gaze that left me with little oxygen in my lungs. "I will never make you regret trusting my loyalty or good intentions when it comes to you and Brooklyn."

Lost for words I offered her a simple nod in return.

"This means you'll have to be the one to take the shot." Samir delivered the nail in my coffin with gloating and grinned crookedly.

A string of curses followed his declaration.

Chapter Seventeen

ALICE

The wolf whined at my feet, pushing his head further into the palm of my hand, begging for scratches. Absently, I rubbed his ear and stared unseeing at the granite kitchen counter where the harsh glare from the recessed lighting bounced off and hit my irises at such an angle it blurred everything around me. The solemnity of my breath brought me to a place of tranquility where there was only silence. No fear, no expectation…

I was floating in a world of oblivion, which suited me just fine.

I had to think.

Laughing Crow was very vague about the details of the ritual, so naturally I was on edge. Normally, I had no problem jumping head first into whatever situation we were facing, but this was different. This time too much was at stake. All I had to do was mess up one thing and my friend could die.

I could kill her.

Tremors raked my body and I shivered uncontrollably.

"You are cold." Samir draped a blanket over my shoulders seemingly out of thin air. All I could do was stare like an idiot at him. "We don't feel the temperature the way humans do. I heard your teeth chattering, so I brought this…" Avoiding my gaze, awkwardly he flicked his fingers at the soft throw wrapped around me.

"Thank you." It felt inadequate but I had no idea what else to say. What do you say to a guy that looks too good for your well-being but is older than your great, great grandmother? And why on earth was I thinking about Samir and how hot he looked?

My heart skipped a beat… okay, fine, it skipped a few of them when my glasses started sliding down my nose and without a second thought he pushed them up for me. His finger grazed the bridge of my nose and I bit on the inside of my cheek so I didn't make a sound. I managed to choke down the whimper, or so I thought. Unfortunately, everyone in the damn house had super-sonic hearing and three pairs of eyes focused on my reddening face.

"Have you heard of personal space?" Scowling at the dude, I smacked his hand away with one hand while clutching the cloudlike softness of the throw with the other. "Back off Dracula, or I'll get my wolf to bite you."

"Dracula?" Samir mouthed, eyes darting from Dominic to Rowen and back, confusion clouding his features. "I am Samir, human. Do you not remember?"

"She knows your name. Dracula is a fictional creature from legends that the humans created to scare each other." Dominic barked a laugh. "It drinks blood to survive."

"A monster," I clarified for fang boy, in case he missed the point. There was no reason to be mean to Samir, but I had to keep him at a distance somehow.

"Are they all like this?" The Atua sounded perplexed, gazing at me as if he were looking at an alien.

"I believe she fancies you, Samir. I've heard of human females and how they act around a male they find suitable for a mate." Rowen snickered while I gaped at him mortified. He stopped immediately as soon as I told the room we could use him as a bait for Brooklyn. Everyone in the room had at least a zero point one percent chance to survive an encounter.

Everyone apart from Rowen that is.

"You just keep talking smack, choir boy. Brooklyn doesn't know you from Adam." I bared my teeth at the witch. "How much you want to bet she latches on to you like a babe to a tit in less than one second?"

"Do not antagonize her, Rowen." Dominic shot the robe dude a dirty look when he sucked in a breath gearing up to argue with me. "She's unpredictable when she's calm. We don't need any of her antics if we are to capture Brooklyn."

"Right." Samir clapped his hands in a symbolic way of cutting off any nonsense. "We know that Brooklyn can sense a familiar scent over a block away in a city like Chicago. We need to figure out how to confuse her senses long enough to lure her as close as possible before she realizes that the scent belongs to Alice. I can stay with the human to assure her safety if things do not go to plan while Rowen awaits our signal to bring around the transportation vehicle. Furthermore, we must make sure she doesn't know Dominic is near."

The wolf, who was lazily swishing his tail up to that point, perked up with Samir's last words. Abruptly, he rose to his feet and padded toward Dominic while the shifter was too busy having a silent conversation with the other two men in the room. I never understood why men did that, but I never understood men in general so there was that. Before anyone could stop him, the wolf's hind leg was cocked to the side and he wheezed all over Dominic's leg, soaking up his jeans almost to the knee.

With a shout of outrage, the shifter jumped back, staring open mouthed at the canine.

"Oh my god, you are a genius." Seeing murder before it happened was a real thing. I felt it at that moment, so I jumped to prevent it. Dropping the throw, I rushed to the wolf and hugged him to me. "Who's a good boy? You are! Yes, you are." All the while pushing his body behind mine and away from the very pissed off feline.

"Alice, step away from the scum, I don't want to hurt you." Dominic snarled over us, his large body casting us in a shadow. "I will skin you now, prick." He stared daggers at my wolf.

"Don't you dare hurt him, cat man. He just gave us the answer we needed. We can use him to mask your scent. All he needs to do is pee on you. It's what hunters do when they hunt deer."

I desperately looked at Samir and Rowen hoping they'd confirm the validity of my claims. Unfortunately, they were too busy trying not to swallow their tongues while holding back laughter. Red faced, they both pounded on their chests like gorillas so I focused my attention back on the angry man hovering over me with clenched fists.

Truth be told, I had no idea if that's why the wolf peed on Dominic. But regardless of the motivation, he still gave us a solution to our problem, so I decided to roll with it.

"I'm serious, Dominic. Brooklyn will never guess you're near if we cover your scent like this. Don't you want to bring her home so we can help her?"

"I do." My sigh was premature because he continued talking. "Right after I kill that coward that's using a human as a shield."

To make matters worse, the wolf growled from behind me.

Without thinking, I turned around and smacked him on the snout.

Samir roared out a laugh followed by Rowen. I was too stunned by my actions to do anything but gape at the wolf.

"You don't get to be cocky while I'm trying to save your life," I hissed at my pet. "I've seen him rip limbs from vampires without breaking a sweat. Trust me, you don't want him to get a hold of you when he's this angry."

Dominic was panting in futile attempts to calm himself down so I stood up to better hide the wolf from his sight. He kept his gaze locked on mine and I matched my breathing to his so I could help him out. It worked with cats I'd rescued when they were scared or upset, so I had nothing to lose.

"How about we go downtown and scout out the area we want to use?" Keeping my tone soothing and even, I tentatively reached out and rubbed his arm with smooth long strokes. "Maybe other ideas will pop out when we see the buildings and everything else around. We'll know what we have to work with."

"The human is right." Samir finally took control of himself and stopped laughing. "We should map out and choose the area wisely that we will be using to apprehend Brooklyn."

"Gee, thanks." My drawl puckered his eyebrows, much to my delight. "I'm as intelligent as you, if not more. I'm not a monkey, you ape."

A scary low type of a growl was still vibrating in

Dominic's chest, so I turned away from the vampire for the sake of keeping all of us in one piece.

"The mongrel stays here," Dominic said through clenched teeth promising painful things to my wolf through narrowed gaze. "I can't guarantee I won't kill him otherwise."

"Sure." I squeaked, freaked out a little by the rage-filled unblinking stare he was giving me, as well. "The wolf stays here. Got it."

"I'll meet you all in the garage." The shifter took a slow deliberate step back and kicked off his boots. "First, I must put on another pair of pants."

With that, he turned around, yanked on his jeans, sending metal buttons flying everywhere before dropping them in a pile around his feet. He walked out of them with the next step and strode across the kitchen while I couldn't look away from his bare ass. The moment he disappeared through the doorway, I audibly swallowed and finally blinked.

"Brooklyn is a lucky girl." A nervous giggle bubbled out before I could stop it. "I bet you can bounce a quarter on that."

Rowen snickered, but Samir stayed silent. I glanced at him over my shoulder and a rock dropped in my belly from the intensity of his eyes. Something primal lurked in his irises, and it made me feel like I was the one standing naked in front of him.

That time I couldn't stop the whimper. I was royally screwed.

Chapter Eighteen

DOMINIC

The human was right. I knew it, she knew it, they all knew it. Just because it didn't sit well with me didn't mean that the idea was not a perfect solution to our problem. My beast fumed just from the thought of the mutt marking us with his urine and wanted to burst out so it could go kill him. I obviously resisted.

For now.

I had to think about Brooklyn and what was best for her.

"I do not think placing the human in harm's way is a very wise action." Samir intercepted me in the hallway. With folded arms, he blocked my path toward the stairway leading to the garage. "Brooklyn entered the cages, something she swore to never allow, so she could save your life and the human's. If the Council get their hands on you two, we will have bigger problems."

"I don't know about you, Samir, but my mate's life is more important to me. We all have our priorities." With a firm shove on his shoulder, I sent him backpedaling into the bust sculpture displayed on a sand colored column.

"I thought we were past the barbaric ways of interaction," he yammered, cradling the bust to his chest like a lover. One of his eyebrows arched up when I smirked as I walked by him. "Alice also mentioned that Brooklyn will need witch's blood freely given after she's drained. The human is offering her own, claiming she has magic."

That made me pause.

"Will it work?" Turning to face him, I tugged at my hair in frustration. "This is all my fault. I should've protected Brooklyn instead of assuring everyone else was safe that night."

"We can reminisce about what could've or should've happened but that won't help us now." Grazing the stone breast with his fingers, Samir grinned at my scowl. "We can always offer Rowen's blood to be sure."

"Will he be willing?" I asked, not trying to mask the doubt in my tone. No witch in their right mind would bare a jugular to an Atua if they could help it.

"If he's not, I can make him be willing. Brooklyn would be a safer option for his throat than me." A slow, humorless smile curled one side of his mouth, revealing a tip of a fang under his upper lip. "I can be very convincing when I need to be."

"That, I believe." Despite myself, I laughed. "Let's go. The sooner we figure out all the details the sooner we can set everything in motion."

"Rowen and the human are awaiting our arrival in the garage." Samir grimaced. "Why is it so strange?"

"What's strange?" Although I asked the question I had an inkling about his problem.

"The human." He huffed in annoyance.

"If she hears that you call her *it*, you'll learn that humans can be deadly, too." Snorting at the male's bewildered expression, I took pity on him. "Magic or not, Alice is a strange creature, I'll give you that. I can see why she intrigues you. She's also kind and loyal. Stay away from her, Samir. One way or another I will get Brooklyn back, and she won't be pleased if a hair is missing from the human's head."

Samir stayed silent all the way to the vehicle, and on the ride to downtown Chicago. Everyone was too silent, which only amped up the tension thickening the air. My mind raced with options and possibilities, but I kept glancing at the Atua as well. He was lost in thought after our short conversation about Alice. I really wanted to tell him about the human's magic but something told me to wait. First, we needed Brooklyn back to her normal self, then we can decide what to share with Samir.

The city was a blur on the other side of the passenger window as we raced through the streets of Chicago. Occasionally, I'd feel a prickle of awareness, and when I locked eyes with Samir, who was driving, he would nod to confirm my suspicion. Atua were in the area. The Syndicate was out in full swing, too. Brooklyn made them chase their own tail probably. If I wasn't worried sick about her, I'd have been proud of my mate.

"If you make a left here, we can stop at a warehouse Brooklyn and I used as a meeting point." Alice spoke from the back seat before her head popped out between me and Samir. "Using a place she is familiar with to capture her, might trigger some memories that could work in our favor. Aka, me not ending up like a juice box."

"That could work in our favor, although I have not heard of anyone remembering anything in the middle of bloodlust." Samir muttered under his breath, pointedly avoiding looking at the human. The steering wheel groaned under his grip.

Alice squeaked when the car made a sharp left turn and stared daggers at the side of the Atua's face. "Down about half a block on your left. You can't miss it. It's the tallest square building... Ohhh my god!" she breathed just as my heart rate sped up.

Samir slowed down the vehicle to a crawl as Rowen sucked in a breath. All we could do was stare mutely at the massacre spread like a red carpet in front of us. It must've just happened because the rain didn't get a chance to wash the blood off the street. There was not one whole body in sight. Body parts littered the pavement, along with the chain-link fences where they dangled in a display of very realistic Halloween decorations.

"Is that a rope?" Alice rasped, gagged, then swallowed audibly. "Please tell me..."

"I believe those are intestines." Tilting his head, Rowen pressed his nose to the glass, fogging it with his breath. "Yes, it's definitely intestines." The witch went as far as giving me a contemplative nod while I stared dispassionately at him and at the scene.

"I think I'm going to puke," she mumbled through the fingers of the hand she was pressing over her mouth.

"It is safe to say our Brooklyn might still be here." Samir swerved smoothly and parked the car on the side of the road. Without a pause, he opened the door and was out with me right on his heels. "I'll take the roofs if you take the alleys."

"Go." I said, and instead of following his lead, I walked back to the black sedan.

When I opened the back door, two sets of eyes as wide as saucers blinked at me.

"Dominic?" Alice whispered from next to the witch, and my gut tightened at the vulnerability in her voice. The human had been tough through everything we'd faced so far. It didn't sit well to see her afraid from one of us. "It was her, wasn't it? Brooklyn did this?"

"She is not herself at the moment, Alice. We both know she's sick." Crouching to bring myself more at her eye level I reached across Rowen and petted her arm. I hoped by using her name she'd understand how serious the situation is. "I need you to stay in the car with Rowen and not come out no matter what you see or hear. Especially if you see Brooklyn. Can you promise me this?"

"No." As honest as always, she perked up a bit from her slouch. "What if I can get her to remember me, Dominic. We can take her back to the house with us now instead of…" The rest was mumbled behind Rowen's palm.

"Your friend is Atua with impressive hearing. Let's not share things we don't have to in case she is indeed around," he told her, and she nodded in understanding with no further argument.

"We stick to the plan," I reminded them both. "Stay here. I'll help Samir do a check of the perimeter and we will be back. Do not exit the vehicle at any cost. Rowen, move behind the wheel and be ready."

Trusting them to do the right thing, I shifted in less time than it took to straighten from my crouch. My body bent and twisted, elongating to accommodate my animal. A feral cry echoed across the street when my senses sharpened and the scent of fresh blood filled my nostrils. Amid the copper, heavy stench of wet pavement, fumes and charged ozone from the gathering lightning in the sky, my mate's natural sweet scent was a punch in the chest.

She was near and not moving away.

A rumbling purr built in my chest, and I released a call for my mate with a terrifying cry. My ear swiveled when a husky laugh reached me from an alley nearly at the end of the block. She knew I was here and she was waiting for me.

I could do nothing else but go to my mate.

Chapter Nineteen

ALICE

Wiggling forward, I jammed my elbows in the two front seats with my heart beating so fast it felt like it was punching at the roof of my mouth. Brooklyn was probably close and I wanted to go find her so bad it hurt. Instead, I gnawed at my lower lip debating on how to trick Rowen so he didn't scream bloody murder if I exited the car. Cat man wouldn't be happy if I didn't follow his orders.

"Maybe we should roll down the street in case they need us," I started, but Rowen was already shaking his head. "We don't need to start the car, I'll push us into a roll. Honest." When he turned to glare at me, I smiled sweetly. "When they need our help and we are not there, you'll feel really stupid. You'll see."

"That's fine. I'd prefer to be stupid than to be dead." He told me flatly. "Last time I listened to you, we ended up running for our lives from a spirit possessed shaman. We are staying here."

"Oh yeah?" Shoving the glasses up my nose with a forefinger, I got as close to him as possible. "Well next time if you put pants on like a normal person instead of robes like a medieval wizard you may run faster too. She almost zapped us multiple times because you tripped twice on all that fabric."

Whatever else was going to come out of my mouth was cut short from a bone rattling roar by a large animal. Deep down I knew it was Dominic but that didn't help my monkey brain to comprehend it. Goosebumps pebbled my skin and I stiffened, pressing my thighs together so I didn't end up peeing myself. I'd never hear the end of it otherwise, I was sure.

"I think they found her." Rowen muttered under his breath, leaning forward on the steering wheel. You'd think, somehow, he would develop night vision and penetrate the darkness in front of us. He totally ignored my jab about the way he dressed.

Hang on one second. "Can you see in the dark?" A deaf person could hear the envy in my tone.

"No," robe dude answered absently, still straining forward toward the windshield.

"Oh." All my indignation deflated immediately. "Never mind then. I still think you need to change your ensemble if you are going to be my sidekick."

That warranted Rowen's attention like nothing else so far. "Sidekick?" His eyes were eerily colorless in the light of the dashboard when he looked over his shoulder at me. Just the pupil stood out like a black dot.

"Yes, sidekick." Flinching at another roar and what sounded like a building collapsing, I continued talking, tremulously bouncing my left knee up and down. I would've cried otherwise. "You decided to tag along for this adventure when I went to visit the shaman. You better be committed now until we finish the job and have Brooklyn back. Which makes you Robin to my Batman."

"Do you often prattle like this when you are nervous?" His tone was earnest, and he studied me with interest.

"I don't know if you've noticed, Rowen, but there are dismembered bodies sprinkled like parsley all over this street. If I'm not nervous, then there is something seriously wrong with me." Sliding my glasses up with one finger, I inhaled deeply. "Internally, I'm screaming to tell you the truth. Nervous is an understatement."

A loud honk of a horn came from somewhere in the distance and my whole body jerked from the unexpected sound. Police sirens accompanied it next, joined by a few more and they were moving closer by the second. New type of urgency started clawing at me but there was no sign of Dominic or Samir.

"I think we need to start moving," I told the witch as I crawled my way to the passenger seat and erratically yanked on the seatbelt. It was jammed for whatever reason, and I couldn't even thread my arm through it. "If the cops come we will have a whole new problem to deal with. Not sure about you, but I'm not taking responsibility for this massacre."

The wailing of the sirens moved closer. My eyes bounced from body parts littering the street to those dangling from roofs of buildings visible in the light cast from the streetlamps. Pointedly avoiding the intestines stretched across the chain-link fence like a chintzy tinsel, I redoubled my efforts and continued jerking and yanking on the seat-belt. The damn thing wouldn't budge to save my life.

A shadow darted between the stop sign across the street

on our left and the parking lot of the abandoned warehouse next to it. Fear washed over me in a wave amplifying the sound of rushing blood in my ears. My surroundings and everything in it were moving fast and in slow motion at the same time, lifting the short hairs on my neck up.

"Rowen." I hissed his name in a warning through gnashing teeth. "Move. Now."

The witch finally snapped out of whatever trance he was in and reached for the start button when the back door was ripped open. My scream could've shattered the glass. Thankfully it didn't and we also stayed alive because Samir slid into the back seat. You'd think he'd been out on a stroll.

"We can pick Dominic up down the block." The vampire told us, tilting his chin up to point the way. "The humans caught whiff of the deaths it seems. Their enforcers are on the way."

I gaped at him.

"Are you well?" Samir's perusal was like a physical touch as he checked me for injuries.

"Did you find Brooklyn?" It was like pulling teeth with your bare hands to get information out of these guys.

"She evaded our efforts to intercept her as I knew she would."

Rowen finally started the car and rolled down the street. Acid filled my mouth when we rocked up and down over the limbs spread over the pavement. We all pretended it wasn't body parts that made our heads bob in the vehicle.

"It also confirmed that we must hide Dominic's scent. She knows where he is at all times." Samir slammed the door closed and leaned back on a sigh. "Luckily for me, or I would've become part of the macabre display."

"I never thought I'd be afraid of Brooklyn, but I must

say I'd rather get out of here," I admitted to them for the first time.

The longer I watched the faint drizzle mix with all the blood covering the street, the further away from the place I wanted to be. The Brooklyn I knew would never allow something like that to happen in her city, much less be the one to cause it. Whatever poison they used made sure my friend was not in her right mind. Not that I was rethinking my part in our plan to capture her, but I would be a fool if I was not scared.

Whatever was jamming the seatbelt released its hold on it and I managed to wrap it around me in time for it to prevent me from headbutting the dashboard. It bit into my shoulder and hip when Rowen slammed on the brakes and we all stared at the unnaturally large panther who was baring his teeth at us from the other side of the windshield. Electric green irises too bright to belong to an animal, Dominic made eye contact with each of us separately.

"He's bleeding." Robe dude swallowed thickly, squeezing the steering wheel in a white knuckled grip.

The police sirens were getting louder.

"Unless his internal organs are falling out and we need to collect them, he needs to get his ass in the car like right now." Panic was clawing at me not just from Brooklyn but the cops too. Dominic cried out at me loud enough to be heard through closed doors. "Hiss all you want, cat man, we gotta go."

I watched the line of police cars pile up at the entrance of the block just as we took a curve and disappeared from sight. If Dominic didn't shift back when he did, they would've seen us. Some third sense was telling me that we were being watched anyway, but when I ducked my head and stared at the roofs, I couldn't see anyone there. It didn't mean my intuition was wrong. It just meant whoever was watching us run away didn't want to be seen.

"I miss you." I mouthed through the window, hoping if it was Brooklyn, she might actually understand that I know it's not her fault and that I missed my friend.

Chapter Twenty

DOMINIC

"Why exactly are we here now?" Alice grumbled for the second time, fearfully craning her neck and looking around like she was expecting someone to attack us in the middle of the day.

"Move." I pushed her forward toward the entrance of the building we needed to infiltrate. "Walk more, talk less."

"Last time I checked we can still go to jail for breaking and entering." Planting her feet stubbornly, she turned to face me. "Why can't we just use the roof like normal people? You're complicating things because you refuse to let my wolf pee on you."

"For the last time, human, I will kill him if he tries to pull that shit again." Taking hold of her upper arm, I propelled her forward while she wiggled like an eel. "This is not complicating anything. Unless we take her by surprise, Brooklyn will either run away or end up killing all of us. Taking a shot from the roof is too obvious and not an option. She'll know I'm there from a block away if not more."

My shoulder throbbed in response to my comment. The night before, I managed to corner my mate in an alley. In truth, she led me there and I took the bait. Good news was she only toyed with me but as a result I lost quite a bit of blood and a chunk of muscle at my shoulder. How many more times would she let me get away before she tired of playing games and went in for the kill? The mate scent could keep me alive for only so long. It was shocking she could control herself as much as she did while in mindless bloodlust.

"There is crime tape everywhere," Alice hissed at me, bending backward and craning her neck to watch the police officers on the other side of the parking lot mingle with passersby.

"I do not care. Why will they bother us about it?"

"Because we were here last night? Because we know who did it?" The female poked me in the ribs with her forefinger with each question. "Pick your poison."

"How will they know we were here last night?"

"They don't need to know," she told me and rolled her eyes. "*I* know we were here."

"You make no sense, human."

"I'm a woman. It's my job not to make sense to you." Snorting a laugh, she shook her head. "Stop dragging me along. I'm not a rag doll. I can walk on my own two feet." My doubt for her claims must've been obvious because she huffed in frustration. "I'll walk on my own, let go."

"Don't make me regret allowing it. If we set up everything now, all we need to do is take positions tonight. Everything will go smoothly and it won't take long." Taking hold of the metal handle, I crushed it in my fist when we reached the side door of the building. "I want you to know where I need Brooklyn to be so I can have a clear shot. That's why you're here."

"That way you can take a keyring shot, right?" Pushing her glasses back to the bridge of her nose, she scrunched her face up.

"Keyhole shot." I corrected her and nudged her to walk through the now open door. "Yes. It's important that we get it right on the first try. I doubt Brooklyn will let us corner her a second time."

"And you're absolutely sure she won't listen to us? We can't talk her into coming home so we can help her?"

If I had any strength left to lie to myself and Alice, I would've entertained her hope. As things stood, I didn't. I was tired to the bone marrow and I needed my mate back. How I'd deal with that fact was something I'd had to think on. When there were no dead bodies decorating Chicago and I wasn't ready to vomit just thinking about her alone and in bloodlust chasing Syndicate members. I had no delusion that Isiah and Frederic forgot about my mate.

I bet they were trying to capture, or kill her.

My blood was boiling in my veins.

"If we can tie her up, I'm sure we can force her to come where we want her to go. We are talking about Brooklyn here, Dominic," Alice persisted, still hopeful that her friend could be saved in another way.

Like I didn't want to just tell the stubborn female to come home. It worried me that Alice would try to pull some stunt at the last minute and screw up our perfectly planned capture. I was ready to throttle the human if she even breathed the wrong way on this.

"Are you willing to risk Brooklyn's life or one of ours to test that?" In case she'd forgotten what happened the night before, I pointedly looked at my shoulder.

"No," Alice mumbled with a flinch. "I just don't like the idea of shooting her, that's all."

"We are tranquilizing her, not shooting her. This is all to help her. Do you honestly believe I can hurt Brooklyn?" I asked at the end of the long hallway as I pushed the exit door leading to the stairs wide open, gesturing for the human to walk in first.

And for some dumb reason, I held my breath, too, waiting on her answer.

"You?" Alice gasped as if personally offended by the question. "Never. Why would you even ask. It's the four of us against everyone else as far as I'm concerned. It's not you that I'm worried about." Shuffling close to the open door, she leaned in carefully to peek through it. "It's clear," she told me with a firm nod.

Silently I led her to the third floor, down the hall to the fourth door on our left. The building belonged to a business and that was the one office no one had used for a while. It was perfect for what we needed. Luring Brooklyn to the warehouse she and Alice used as a meeting point was a smart decision. A familiar place regardless that Brooklyn didn't understand why. She even did her macabre decorating on that very street.

Alice followed behind me, warily observing our surroundings. She raised an eyebrow when I pulled out my glass cutting tool and cut out a small section of the window but wisely stayed silent. The office was scarcely furnished too, which suited me just fine, and it gave her space to move around without bumping into anything.

Leaning down, I eyed the parking lot across the street from the cut out in the window. The dart would need to pass through the hole, between two branches of one tree on our side of the road, miss a stop sign in front of the chain-link fence then go through a chain-link to reach Brooklyn.

It was doable if Alice made sure they were in the right spot.

"Come here, human." I urged her to join me at the window.

"You know if you call me by my name, I'll be more inclined to do what you need," she drawled. "Like this I just want to be a jerk to piss you off."

"Do I need to remind you why we are here?" Cocking a brow, I waited.

"Yeah, yeah." Flicking her hand left and right in my face, Alice rolled her eyes. "I'm here, now what?"

Placing my hand on top of her head, I lowered her slightly until she was eye level with the hole I cut in the window. The clothing she was wearing was too big on her so she lifted her arms up and wiggled them to make the sleeves reveal her hands. After she pressed both palms on the glass, she turned to face me very slowly.

"I hope you are aware that even with my glasses I can't see past that green car in the parking lot," Alice informed me. "Did you bring binoculars?"

"No." I snarled.

It's not like I was upset with Alice. None of it was her fault. I was angry at myself for expecting her to be anything but a human. The urge to punch something was too strong.

"It's okay, cat man." She straightened and patted me on the chest. I had a feeling she thought it was a soothing gesture although it was anything but. It was agitating me to no end. "Tell me what I can do to help you here if you have to do anything else. After that, just show me the exact spot Brooklyn needs to occupy across the street. I'll make sure she stands there. Promise. "

Unable to hold a conversation with my animal so close to the surface, I nodded in answer. What was always extraordinary about Alice however was her ability to understand me better than I understood myself. She claimed it was my animal that made sense to her, not me.

She helped me align a file cabinet and the desk in perfect positions before we left the building. Silently, we both worked and exited through the side door within minutes. It wasn't until we reached the parking lot across the street that Alice spoke.

"This might not work, huh?" Lifting her face up, she blinked owlishly at me, the thick glasses making her eyes look too big for her face. "I could die tonight. Brooklyn might kill me."

"She will never hurt you." The conviction was lacking in my tone, but Alice started nodding before I finished talking.

"No. I know she will never hurt me." Her lip wobbled when she offered me a smile. "This is our Brooklyn we are talking about. She's stronger than any poison. She's stronger than this."

"Yes." I didn't look Alice in the eye when I agreed with her. I couldn't, because it was a lie.

The chances were, Brooklyn might kill all of us tonight.

It'd been a very long time since I prayed to any god hoping that I was doing the right thing, but it was never too late to start.

I did pray that night.

Chapter Twenty-One

ALICE

Misty clouds puffed up in front of my face with each breath I took. It was freezing outside and yet I was sweating bullets under my borrowed jacket. One of these days when I wasn't dealing with one disaster after another, or I was not preoccupied with finding ways of how not to die, I would be planning a shopping spree. And I'd buy everything I needed in my size, damn it. Not to be misunderstood, I didn't mind the oversized clothing. On the contrary, it was actually comfy as hell.

Plus, I figured if I was about to die I'd rather go down cozy as a snuggle bug instead of squeezed in spandex sucking in my gut. Take that, Universe!

Samir cleared his throat from somewhere behind me to remind me I was fidgeting too much or something like that, but I pointedly ignored him, obviously. That guy had some serious issues when it came to personal space or boundaries. Instead of giving in to the urge of saying something just to annoy him, I ducked my head lower and burrowed my face in the lifted collar of the jacket. Up until an hour ago I was all bravado, mouthing off as usual, ready as I'd ever be to get this over and done with.

Not so much when I stood in a dark parking lot in the middle of the night.

Nope, I was twitchy as fuck and ready to bolt. I knew what was out and about when the sun went down now, and I wanted nothing to do with any of them. Well, apart from Brooklyn, which was why I was rooted to the spot. The fear only made me feel like the soles of the Italian dress shoes three sizes too big were glued to the pavement.

I had every intention of bolting out of the damn place barefoot like my ass was on fire if it came down to it. I'd be kicking these mofo's off like yesterday's news.

"Act normal, human," Samir hissed from the darkness way above my head.

"Normal how? Like a lamb that accidentally walked into a wolf's den or like a pig stepping up in front of a butcher?" There was no need to wonder if he could hear my muttering. I felt his intent glare burning a hole on top of my head with each word I spoke.

Samir didn't make further comments, and I did the adult thing and no longer jerked around like a skittish rabbit. Deep down, I knew Brooklyn would never hurt me if she was in her right mind. If I were honest with myself, I'd say she wouldn't do it even if she was out of her own mind.

It wasn't her that worried me.

A crunch of gravel boomed like a bullet being fired next to my ear in the eerily silent street. Surprisingly, the distant hum of traffic and honking horns did nothing to calm my frayed nerves. Usually, Chicago had this buzz about it no matter how quiet everything was. Like the city itself was alive and purring, a sleeping giant allowing us to take a ride on its back.

Not that night.

I clenched my teeth so they didn't chatter and trembled uncontrollably. Everything in me was screaming for me to run. My instincts were urging me to make a mad dash and sprint for as long as my legs would carry me until I could no longer stand or even breathe. Locking my knees, I forced myself to stand still.

"You can do this, Alice," I told myself firmly under my breath. "Brooklyn would do the same for you."

If asked, I wasn't sure I'd be able to answer how I knew the moment they stepped into the parking lot. Unlike my closest circle, I couldn't feel the power of the supernatural beings. My hearing and my sense of smell were that of a human, yet I could've sworn I tasted the ozone flavor of their etherealness on my tongue. Goosebumps pricked my skin, and I pressed my legs closer in case my bladder decided to give out on me. I wasn't gonna lie, I was ready to pee myself when I heard the low menacing chuckle from right behind me.

"What are you doing alone in this part of town?" a deep male voice murmured in my ear from right behind me. I didn't hear the bastard approach. "Anything can happen to a pretty little girl at night."

"You don't say," I drawled because I had no idea what to do that did not involve screaming my head off. Impressively, my snark was confident and even. I couldn't even tell that I was shaking in my shoes with how calm I sounded. "Let me guess, all that could happen to a girl alone is you. Am I right, or am I right?"

Dominic was a block away, I reminded myself, and he was not a human. I might not survive it, but at least he would kill them for touching me and messing up his plan to get Brooklyn back. That was dumbly comforting. His supernatural hearing made sure he could hear every word spoken and I whispered a quick thank you just in case I didn't get a chance to say it to him otherwise.

On principle, I didn't want to trust that the vampire on top of the warehouse would come to my rescue although he was much closer. We expected someone to intercept me when we made our plans but talking about it and living through it proved to be very different. I didn't want Samir's help, but if it'd be better to not mess up our carefully organized capture, I'd take it. Especially when an ice-cold fingertip traced a line on the back of my neck.

To my embarrassment, I squeaked like a frightened little girl, shrinking away from my tormentor. The jerk laughed.

It pissed me off.

"You are seriously so tough, scaring a woman in a dark parking lot. You should be very proud of yourself." Spinning around, I took a couple of steps away from whoever was behind me and ended up facing the bully nose to bare chest. My glasses started sliding down my nose, yet my hands hung limply to my sides, unable to lift so I could push the frame back up.

Slowly, I looked up until my gaze locked on a pair of soulless black eyes.

I peed a little then.

I'd seen these guys before. Guardians for the Syndicate. According to Brooklyn, they were brainless minions doing the Council's bidding, but looking at the bare-chested dude that close told me otherwise. Evil stared back at me through those abyss eyes and he was giving off a weird vibe that made my soul shrink back inside my being.

Something was terribly wrong with the man. Male. Whatever the hell he was.

A slow, revolting smile curled his lips, exposing the tips of two fangs under his upper lip. It took me back to my dad's safe house the night the Syndicate attacked us en-masse, destroying everything. My heart rate skyrocketed, jackhammering in my throat so hard it was easy for him to hear. I found it difficult to breathe which made the psycho tremendously happier.

"You are a pretty little thing, aren't you?" He took a step forward, I took a step back. "Lucky too that it was me who found you. I might not kill you immediately."

"How very comforting." That time the crippling fear was evident in the trembling of my voice.

With a chuckle, the guardian reached a meaty hand to grab me, so I ducked, dived on his right and rolled away from him. Heart in my throat, I scrambled back on my feet and flipped around to keep him in sight. Where was Rowen when you needed him. Robe dude would've been of great help just by being nearby.

A second guardian stepped in the light of the street lamp, glowering at us. "We have a task to complete," he addressed his buddy with no further explanation.

"The hunt will be more pleasant with some destruction," the first guardian replied with his head cocked to the side as he eyed me curiously. "Does she not look familiar to you?"

"The female is a human. Food. They all look the same to me." The second dude sounded like such a ray of sunshine I wanted to give him a hug.

With both hands wrapped around his neck. And squeeze. Like, really hard.

Where the hell was Samir and why wasn't he removing these two away from me?

For a moment the craziest idea crossed my mind. That although Samir and Dominic mentioned the Syndicate might get involved in our attempt to capture Brooklyn, they never intended to help me if it happened. Dominic was so desperate to get his hands on my friend that he'd be willing to sacrifice my life to have her back. He was my friend too, I never doubted that. But if it came between Brooklyn and the rest of the world, Dominic would watch the whole planet burn for her. He would always choose to save her.

Fear clawed at me.

In my distraction, I never saw the guardian move. A hand as cold as ice wrapped around my neck, and I stilled like a mouse caught in a trap. Wide-eyed, I gaped at the monster's smirking face, trembling uncontrollably in his grip. In my desperation to get away from the two guardians and from the horribly terrifying thoughts circling like vultures in my head, I blindly swung my fist. At the same time my leg jerked back and kicked out with all the strength of a person fighting to survive.

I could've sworn I heard his family jewels crack open when the expensive Italian leather shoe slammed between his legs. And because lady luck was finally on my side, the said shoe slid off my foot and flew like a boomerang into the other guardian's face, landing with a loud thud.

My feet were moving before they touched the ground when the grip on my neck was loosened. With a shriek high-pitched enough to shatter glass, I bolted for the warehouse. If Mohammed didn't go to the mountain, the mountain would go to Mohammed.

With a string of very colorful curses, the two guardians stirred behind me. Grunting and spitting vile words, I had no doubt they were about to come at me hard. The short hairs on the back of my neck lifted at attention but that only made me more determined to reach safety at all costs. I'd climb the outside walls if I had to.

"Dominic, you better pray I don't die or I will haunt you for all eternity." I huffed and puffed under my nose, arms pumping hard in my sprinting.

Samir better be ready to defend me, or I'd take his bloodsucking ass down with me.

Chapter Twenty-Two

DOMINIC

I should've known things wouldn't go as planned when Alice was involved.

Truth be told, I couldn't blame her that the Syndicate was out in full swing hunting Brooklyn, but it did annoy the hells out of me to have the plan messed with. Everything in me wanted to abandon position and go protect the human, but if I did that, I had a feeling Brooklyn would show up and everything would go to shit. I didn't want to say it out loud as if I could speak it into existence, but I thought the longer we waited the harder it would be to get Brooklyn back to herself.

The night we went scouting the area before we formulated the plan confirmed my fears. My mate held back from killing me but just barely. There was no playfulness left in her voice and no flicker of her green eyes was to be seen. A lump formed the size of my fist that I couldn't swallow, just thinking how much she had to be fighting her own psyche to stop herself from killing me.

Alice surprised me by sounding very calm in her interaction with the guardian who walked up behind her. The second one was alertly prowling on the edge of the parking lot, scanning the area in case they were walking into a trap, so although I focused on the human, I kept him in sight with the corner of my eye.

With a deep breath, I released the tight hold I had on my senses to check who else was in the vicinity and if Brooklyn was anywhere nearby. Apart from three more guardians a couple of blocks away, nothing else was in this part of Chicago but us. My heart did a hard punch on my rib cage when Alice squeaked in fear. Hand tightening on the handle of the gun, I gnashed my teeth. What in the name of all the gods was Samir doing?

"You are a pretty little thing, aren't you?" The guardian took a step forward, Alice took a step back. "Lucky too that it was me who found you. I might not kill you immediately."

All the ways I would dismember the scum if he hurt her came to mind.

"How very comforting," the human whispered, unable to hide the tremble in her tone.

It really rubbed me wrong that he was scaring her, but maybe it could work in our favor if Brooklyn heard it, so I stayed where I was. My mate couldn't tell a friend from a foe, but she was a female. I held hope that she would want to help another female. I wasn't foolish enough to believe she'd recognize who or what Alice was to her.

Not after our encounter the night before.

"Does she not look familiar to you?" Hearing that from the guardian tormenting Alice snapped me out of my thoughts.

"The female is a human. Food. They all look the same to me." The second one joined them under the yellow glow of the street lamp.

A low growl rumbled in my chest the longer I watched things unfolding a block away with no way of doing anything about it. My molars cracked when the scum lifted the human by the throat, but I couldn't stop myself from snorting a laugh when she kicked him in the balls with all her strength.

"Run, Alice," I said breathily and lifted the tranquilizing gun so I could watch through the scope.

It was now or never, I thought to myself. If Brooklyn didn't show up now, nothing was going to stop me from going to Alice's rescue. I would kill Samir too for sitting there like a lump and not helping her. There was something going on between the two of them, and it could cause a shitstorm one day if they didn't start acting like adults. The fact that I warned Samir off Alice was beside the point.

Closing my eyes, I let my senses be my sight. If I was going to make the perfect shot and capture my mate, I couldn't look through the scope longer than a split second. With only glimpses of Alice running for dear life toward the warehouse and the two guardians rolling on the ground— one holding his nose, the other hugging his balls—I breathed as slow as possible.

Brooklyn must show up any moment now, I told myself so I could stay in my position.

Each inhale took longer, each exhale lasted a heartbeat more.

Everything around me blurred out, the one spot bathed in golden light from the streetlamp coming into laser focus. A leaf fluttered in front of my scope from one of the trees, but I kept my gaze unfocused.

I'd have one chance to help my mate.

Only one.

A scream shattered the silence of the bubble I created

around myself. Like a hammer slammed on top of my head, bringing with it the reality that I was crouched in a somewhat empty room while Alice was probably getting hurt or even killed by the bloodsuckers. What would Brooklyn say or think if her friend was dead when she recovered from the bloodlust? Because there was no other possibility or option. I would be getting her back.

And probably lose her if Alice was dead.

What in all the worlds was I thinking?

Panic speared me through the chest just as a movement pulled my focus at the scope.

Brooklyn.

My mate stepped into a perfect spot, blocking my view of Alice with her back.

Another scream shattered what little logic I had left, so without thinking, I held my breath and pulled the trigger. She started turning her head to look back the second the dart left my rifle with a dull whooshing thump. The tranquilizer dart lodged itself in the side of her neck just as we made eye contact. I knew she couldn't actually see me, but she was looking right at where I was across the block.

"Clever," Brooklyn mouthed, smirking as if she knew it was me who made that shot.

I expected her to crumple down unconscious, and my body was coiled to spring into action. Instead, my mate spun on her heel, and swaying her hips walked into the darkness of the parking lot, yanking the dart out and tossing it over her shoulder.

"Ah, fuck." I sprang to my feet and dashed out the door with the second tranquilizer clutched in a tight grip.

Taking the stairs three at a time, I descended as fast as I could. My boots beat a staccato rhythm on the *pavement* when I sprinted across the block in hopes to reach the warehouse sooner rather than later. My beast roared in my head, pushing me to shift, but I resisted. Cold air bit into my over-heated skin, which helped a little to calm me down. I needed to be logical about this, not act on pure instinct alone.

By the time I reached the parking lot, I knew I was too late for something. There was an oppressive feeling in the air pressing down on me like a giant hand pushing on my shoulders. Dread spread through my insides, chilling me to the bone. The moment I reached the fire-escape of the warehouse building it became apparent why everything felt final.

There was blood everywhere, and at that second, some-thing inside me solidified like a rock. Knowledge drilled into my bone marrow that I'd lost something integral to who I was as a being. With everything in me I dared hope it was not Brooklyn. There would be a whole new hell unleashed in Chicago if I lost my mate.

With a solid jump, I grabbed the metal railing and yanked myself up. Feet barely touching the stairs, I jolted my body forward, panting somewhat with anticipation, but mostly out of fear. All I wanted to do was wrap my arms around my mate and take her away from this damn city. When I reached the roof, I had to stop and blink to realize what I was looking at.

Then I ducked, rolled on the roof and popped back up a few feet away when a dagger slashed at the air where my head used to be.

"Dominic!" Alice shouted, the panic in her voice making it sound almost childlike.

She proceeded to scream shrilly, so I stepped to the side, using an air conditioning unit as a barrier between myself and my attacker. A quick check told me it was the second guardian that tried to skewer me with his dagger while doing his best not to bleed out. One hand pressed firmly to his sternum, he held his intestines inside his gut while slashing blindly with the dagger held in a bloody fist of the other.

Maybe this was not as bad as I feared, I told myself prematurely. Maybe the guardians were the ones sharing their life liquid with the building and the metal railing.

A scream pierced the night.

My head jerked to the side to find Alice spinning both her arms in circles so she could keep her balance on the edge of the roof where she stood on her tiptoes. The glasses dangled from one of her ears, and her eyes were so wide I worried they'd roll out of her face. Brooklyn had one hand wrapped around the human's neck, but she wasn't looking at her friend. She was tracking Samir through a slitted gaze while he circled her. The Atua was bleeding from multiple cuts on his body and there was a chunk of muscle missing from his left biceps.

"Next time I will take your whole arm." Brooklyn snickered at him.

The other guardian was dismembered at her feet. I tasted bile.

"Let the human go, girl. Your quarrel is with me." Samir's tone was clear and firm. If I hadn't been looking at him, I wouldn't have known he was gravely injured.

"Why? Humans are food, are they not?" My mate sneered before pulling Alice closer to her. "Why is this one important to you?"

I'd fought alongside my mate too many times not to know her body language. She was about to kill one, if not both of them, if I didn't do something. I also knew that if she saw me, I might speed up their deaths although she was aware I was on the roof with them.

"She's not important to him." Keeping my tone calm, I stepped out from behind the unit. The second dart was tucked inside my waistband at the small of my back. "That human is important to you."

It was a mistake the moment it came out of my mouth. I could feel Samir's eyes rolling to the back of his head from exasperation, and Alice literally squeaked in fright. The wounded guardian roared and streaked toward the human with one arm outstretched. Samir twisted away from Brooklyn and threw himself between the two females and the male just in time to tackle him to the ground. They rolled away with fists flying and fangs flashing.

My mate's gaze darted between the two fighting Atua, me, and Alice in rapid succession before a decision formed in her head. I saw it the moment it solidified almost like a physical change in Brooklyn. It happened in slow motion although it took a few seconds at best.

Brooklyn turned to face Alice, determination written in every line of her features. Snatching the dart from my back I flung myself at her with everything in me, arm raised above my head. Alice's eyes widened unnaturally, her mouth opened in a silent scream.

"Brooklyn, no!" my bellow echoed around us as I reached my mate and jabbed the second dart between her neck and her shoulder, thumb pressing on the plunger hard enough to hear the needle crunch on a bone.

Everything stopped.

All sound was gone, even the hum of the city and the distant honk of horns stopped.

My heart was not beating for the longest time either.

Brooklyn's head was bent, forehead resting on Alice's

shoulder for the longest second of my life before a whisper broke the suspended bubble.

"Dominic?" Alice rasped, pale as a sheet of paper.

My eyes locked on hers for a flash before my mate twitched and raised her head. Rain started drizzling softly on my face, and I nearly smiled until I realized it wasn't raining.

As soon as Brooklyn lifted her head, blood started spraying from the side of Alice's neck. My mate turned slowly, bleached of color and green eyes wide as plates.

"What have I done?" Brooklyn cried out, ripping my heart to shreds. Her eyes rolled to the back of her head and she crumpled at my feet.

With no one to hold her weight, Alice slipped from Brooklyn's hold and plummeted down toward the parking lot on a shrill scream, hand pressed to the blood spraying from her opened wound. Numbness spread through me because I knew I was not fast enough to catch her so my body reacted on instinct and caught Brooklyn before she hit the ground.

A tortured moan came from my mate, but a shadow passed next to me that got my attention. I looked to the side in time to see Samir jumping off the roof which made me admire the male, albeit begrudgingly. There was no way he could catch Alice, but at least he was male enough to try, unlike me. Another tormented moan from Brooklyn made me glance down where I cradled her in my arms.

"How could you let me do that, Dominic." Tears rolled down her cheeks. I was impressed that she was still awake after the second dose of mercury. "I will never forgive you."

It was a dagger to my heart to hear that, but I didn't regret a second. I'd do it all over again if it meant saving my mate. Even if she hated me for the rest of her life.

A roar of pain echoed in the night, Samir's anger palpable in the punch of power it packed. Dripping from my lashes, a tear rolled down my skin with Alice's face floating in my mind's eye. I should've placed her glasses back where they belonged, I thought distractedly. The silence that followed Samir's pain was too loud.

Until a cheerful sound of an ice cream truck broke it.

In all the rush, I'd forgotten Rowen was tasked to drive in with an ice cream truck to pick up Brooklyn. Alice thought it was the best way to transport her friend with the built-in freezer of the vehicle since we were going to use liquid nitrogen.

Brooklyn was limp in my hold, finally unconscious.

"I'm so very sorry, Alice," I whispered while the pain was unbearable in my chest.

I'd failed everyone again.

Drowning in my misery, I almost missed Samir's shout.

"Hurry up, shifter, she's still alive." The Atua roared for the second time.

Jolted out of my self-inflicted torment, I jumped to my feet, holding Brooklyn to my chest.

"If she dies, Dominic, so will you," Samir barked, and despite everything, I grinned on my way down.

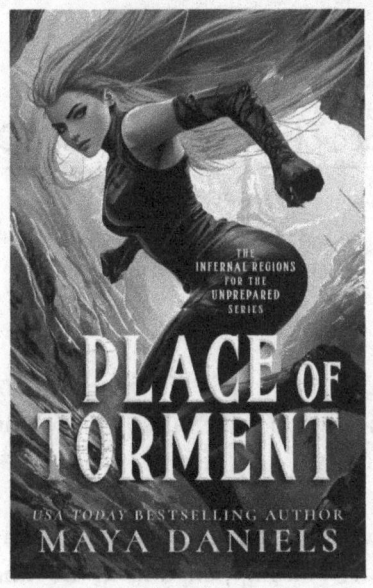

Place of Torment: Chapter One

BROOKLYN

At some point in everyone's life, a person comes to realize that they do believe in fairy tales. The reason for this realization is simple: everyone lies.

And we lie the best to ourselves.

The exact same thing I was currently doing in hopes to justify everything that happened from the moment Veronica was killed until I almost killed Alice in my bloodlust. Every day, every mistake I made flickered and spun behind my mind's eye, taunting me to a point of madness.

I had good intentions for all of it from day one, even when I sought revenge. The gods know I did. We meant well with all our actions, which led us to a point of no return. In our righteousness, we slowly became the monsters we were hunting. A head-spin rocked my body sideways, and the world around me tilted on its axis for a scary second.

I almost killed Alice.

Dominic almost killed Alice by placing her in my path when I couldn't tell a friend from a foe.

All I knew was blood.

I still remembered the gnawing hunger for her blood clawing at the back of my throat.

I remembered the taste too and wished I could die a thousand deaths because saliva immediately pooled in my mouth from the memory.

A tremor zipped from my tailbone to the base of my skull, and I shivered slightly, eyes jumping guiltily from the twisted fingers in my lap to the pale face of my friend, which looked too small nestled in the huge pillows Samir insisted she rest upon. Her sluggish heartbeat spit and stuttered in her chest like the timeworn van her late father left her in case alien monsters attacked the human race.

No outer space creatures came, but he was probably turning in his grave from the fact that she chauffeured monsters around in that rusted can. Behemoths that were a danger to her no matter which way you looked at it. There were no doubts left about what we were anymore.

We were monsters that would've and still could cost her, her life.

In this entire nightmare, she was the only one with the heart in the right place—the only innocent one.

She should've been somewhere safe. I should've made sure of it. All the many would'ves and should'ves circled like vultures through my mind, tormenting me without a pause. I'd go insane if this continued. And we all knew where that led. Everyone I cared about had a front row seat to that one.

"You can't keep doing this to yourself." As if reading my mind, Samir muttered under his breath from his spot against the wall so that only I could hear him. He did it without opening his eyes or lowering his face that he had tilted upward at the high ceiling. "You are coherent enough to be a thorn in the side to all of us but not recovered as much as you should be if the Syndicate comes knocking. You are not doing any favors for any of us if you are weak."

He'd been a permanent fixture next to the bed after he placed Alice on it, growling like a wild beast at anyone who suggested he move. On the opposite side of the ancient Atua, the wolf was stretched out on the floor, his snout propped on his folded front paws with one eye open and the upper lip permanently curled over razor sharp teeth in a snarl as a warning. Everything was as it should be in order to give me that peace of mind that no harm would come to my friend. Yet, guilt gnawed a hole in my stomach, warning me that the threat was here; I just couldn't see it. That if I even dared blink, Death would take her away from me forever the same way it took Veronica.

It took my breath away to realize you could love someone so much that the very feeling would be enough to fuel blinding hatred toward everyone and everything around you that wanted to hurt them. That love was strong enough to make you hate yourself even if you placed them, intentionally or not, in harm's way.

Instead of sharing my epiphany, I pushed it away. Samir needed a lecture on hypocrisy for sharing his wisdom uninvited. "The same way you are not doing us any favors by not sleeping or feeding, you mean? There is no difference if I sit here or in the bedroom three doors down. I'm recovering right in front of you as we speak." Tiredly, I rubbed a hand over my face and grimaced when I looked down at my palm. Crusted blood and dirt flaked off of my skin and floated all over my pants, identifying me as a liar. "You could make yourself useful and bring me a wet washcloth though, if you don't mind." He answered my raised eyebrow with one of his own after he excruciatingly slowly lowered his head to make eye contact. "Or not," I amended bleakly.

His answering snort spoke volumes about my audacity to order him around, but things were different now. We were both different. He was no longer my master nor was I an obedient fool. Not that I'd ever been amenable and subservient. However, that never stopped him from sticking his nose where it didn't belong.

"You can't keep ignoring or avoiding him forever either." We both knew who he was referring to. Holding eye contact, Samir dared me to look away so he could call me a coward for trying my best to avoid the panther shifter. That privilege was afforded only to Alice, so I didn't dare move an eyelash as I stared back at him. Even when the corner of my eye became itchy, you'd think my body was doing things on purpose so that I would lose the staring match with the ancient pain in my butt.

"Since when did you become a country fair fortune teller giving unwanted relationship advice to poor souls?" The knowing glint in his dark eyes that saw way too much made me keep talking so I didn't scratch at my face. "I remember the times when you aspired to provoke fear from everyone around you, not eye rolling." And I proceeded to do just that. I rolled my eyes dismissively.

"I never took you for…" Samir started.

"Don't say it." All unwanted sensations forgotten, I hissed through clenched teeth, my fingernails digging into the palms of my fisted hands. A piece of hair escaped my ponytail, and the red strand licked the side of my face like a flickering flame, just enough to anger me more. I yanked it back behind my ear. "I have never been, nor would I ever be, a coward!"

"Very well." With a mocking smirk, he inclined his head

regally at me and narrowed his gaze. "You have always been logical with both feet rooted to the ground. There is nothing wishy washy in the Brooklyn I know. Everything Dominic did was because he loves you. You know this to be true. He was ready to rip the worlds apart to get you back. You cannot fault him for trying to do even the impossible to save his mate. Realms have been destroyed by males doing what is necessary to protect their mates and keep them safe."

"You think I judge my mate too harshly for his actions? I judge myself more for everything I did, and tainted blood is not a passable excuse for being a remorseless, unrepentant killer." The legs of the chair screeched loudly as they scraped over the wooden floors when I jumped to my feet, fists balled at my sides so I didn't wrap my hands around Samir's neck. "Who died and made him God so that he could decide who lives and who dies? Who?" Tears burned at the back of my eyes and a fist was lodged in my throat, making my voice crack. "We have no right to decide anyone's fate. None of us do. We are monsters!" A treacherous tear rolled over my cheekbone and stubbornly dangled on my jawline long enough for the older male to be able to track it with his eyes.

"Easy now, child." Both hands lifted to the sides, palms facing me in a placating motion, as he pushed off the wall and took a step toward me. "It will take a few more days for the tainted blood to fully release its hold. Rage is still fast to overpower logic. Take a deep breath and stay calm."

All I saw was red while his voice was muted and too far away for me to hear without straining. Somewhere in the back of my mind, I was aware that something was wrong, but I couldn't get a grip on my emotions to save my life. Like slippery silk, they trickled between my fingers to escape my hold.

"Men." The barely audible sound of Alice's voice doused all of my anger with the strength of a bucket of iced cold water, yanking me back to the present with a slingshot, like nothing ever would've been able to. Both Samir and I turned sharply to stare wide-eyed at the human eyeing us dazedly from the mountain of pillows. "A sure way to meet your maker before it's your time to go is to tell a pissed off woman to calm down. It goes as well as trying to pet a cat after keeping her tied in a bag for a couple of days. No offense to Dominic." My friend attempted to make a joke with a forced smile for my benefit, and my heart clenched painfully in my chest at the gammy grimace that twisted her features. "No one told the poor dude that, huh?"

My mouth opened and closed a few times, but my throat was dry, and no sound came out. All of us, including the wolf who raised his head when Alice spoke, stood frozen in disbelief. Her face swam as my eyes filled with tears and traveled unchecked when they trickled down my face. All that I managed was an embarrassing croak before I rushed the bed and collapsed on it with heart wrenching sobs that were ripped from the very center of my being.

"You." With shaking fingers, I latched on to her cold hand. It felt like it was the only thing keeping me from exploding into a million pieces. "Are...awake."

"Oh, Brooklyn." She murmured and tried to squeeze my hand. I only knew this because her fingers twitched and that was all the strength she had. I tightened my hold on her instead, mindful not to break her bones.

"I am, so, so, sorry, Alice!" Sobs kept wracking my hunched shoulders. "This is all my fault. All of it. But I will make it right. I promise you I'll make it right."

"The Syndicate did this, not you." Her voice broke, and she started coughing weakly. Samir was there in an instant, shoving me out of his way and holding her up so he could press a glass of water with a straw to her lips. "None of us...did anything...wrong."

"Shhhh, don't talk." He cooed at Alice like he was hushing a newborn. "Talking can wait for when you are stronger."

He glanced at me quickly to make sure I was paying attention. "She has times where she wakes up for a minute or two, but it costs her dearly." After brushing a strand of hair from her sweaty forehead, he pressed the glass more insistently to her dry, cracked lips. "Sip now, *Esme.*"

I froze, as did he.

Well, well. What do you know.

The ancient Atua recovered quickly and continued his whispering encouragements for Alice to sip the water while I stared stunned at the back of his head. He used the ancient Persian word for beloved to address my friend. My first reaction was to snap his neck—immediately. The second reaction that rose within me had a more permanent consequence that was way too tempting, but I had to shake the urges away. I must've missed a lot of things while blood-lust was behind the wheel driving me all over Chicago.

There was a time and place for everything, I'd learned. So, when Samir glanced at me over his shoulder, his ancient eyes guarded, I gave him a sharp nod to tell him I planned on keeping my mouth shut and staying out of whatever was going on between him and my friend.

For now.

I could always kill him later.

That sounded like a delightful plan if I've ever heard one.

The future was looking brighter by the minute if you asked me.

Place of Torment: Chapter Two

I left Samir to tend to Alice while I walked out into the hallway. I closed the door with a soft click before leaning my forehead against it and shutting my eyes. The cold wood of the door was a much-needed reprieve to my heated skin. A total opposite of other times when my body was a frozen popsicle waiting for spring thaw and I resembled a corpse. My internal temperature was really out of whack since I snapped out of my bloodlust. So I took a deep breath, allowing my shoulders to drop, not worried that anyone would see my weakness. The house was as silent as a tomb —so much so that the rhythm of my heart was echoing too loud in my ears.

I was tired.

Carrying a chip on my shoulder had become second nature, and I didn't notice the weight of it anymore. The guilt and responsibility of those around me, however, was a newly formed burden, which pressed so hard on my shoulders that it made it difficult to walk most days without doubling over. In the last few days or so I had a lot of time to think and reexamine my actions.

I was pretty sure anyone would agree when I said I acted rashly. A million excuses came to mind that could ease my culpability and justify everything. Be that as it may, I refused to use my rage and thirst for revenge as a crutch for placing everyone I cared about in danger. A slip up here and there in the name of a righteous indignation was one thing. But everyone suffering, or God forbid, dying, because I couldn't seem to get a grip on myself was a totally different story.

Enough was enough.

I stood there for hours it seemed, pressing my hands to my cheeks to cool them off and rolling my head all over the door while my mind raced, not wanting to miss the chance to taunt me with everything I'd done wrong. Lost in my thoughts, I didn't notice when the energy around me shifted, thickening the air and making it pregnant with tension. It spoke volumes about my current state and how much I needed to lie down so I could fully recover.

Not that I'd do it.

But it was telling.

"You are not feeling well?" Dominic asked but didn't approach me. It cost him dearly to keep his distance now that we'd opened Pandora's box by acknowledging the mate bond we so expertly avoided all this time.

"I'll be all right." My lips grazed the now warmed up wood of the door when I answered, keeping my eyes closed still so I didn't tempt myself to turn around and rush into his arms.

My whole being was tense, coiled like a rusted spring waiting to snap at the slightest brush of a breeze. There was no way in all hells that he didn't notice the slight tremor of my fisted hands or the coppery scent of my blood pooling in the small crescent cuts my nails left in my palms. Still, I stayed glued to the spot as if that would keep me away from the tsunami of emotions threatening to overwhelm me.

"Brooklyn, we can't keep doing this to each other." His voice came from much closer, although I didn't hear him move. Damn cats and their stealth. The hurt from my rejection was evident in the slight rasp of his tone and it took all the energy I had left not to visibly shiver. "You can be angry with me, hate me if that is what you want, but I don't and will not regret my actions. Ever."

My fist was lodged in my throat, closing it effectively up; and I swallowed thickly in hopes it would go down and I'd tell Dominic to leave me alone. Instead, my body began to quiver, and much to my embarrassment, my knees gave out.

That was all the signs he needed. He was there in an instant, scooping me up before I made contact with the floor. His male scent surrounded me from all sides, wrapping me tightly into a Dominic cocoon. My nose was full of him, my head was swimming from the fast pumping of blood my brain received while my heart jackhammered behind my ribcage with the strength of a tornado.

He was warm. Too warm under my clammy fingers that clung to any part of him I could reach like a lifeline. No matter how hard I wanted to push him away, scream at him that he almost killed Alice, my body had a mind of its own. I was acutely aware of every inch where he connected with me. The hard expanse of his muscled body molded to my smaller frame as he curled inward, as if he was trying to absorb me inside of him so that I could never get away. And I let him, curling firmly into his chest, my knees almost touching my chin.

Samir nagged that I couldn't avoid the shifter forever,

but this was the very reason why I'd been like a skittish mouse racing through the hallways of the enormous house, hoping I wouldn't run into him around every corner. I knew once he had his hands on me it would be game over.

Heat bloomed in my lower belly, and arching my back in his hold, I pressed my mouth onto his. A sharp intake of breath was the only sign that he never expected the situation to go in that direction, but he recovered quickly, and his warm wet tongue parted my lips with the desperation of a man dying from thirst faced with a glass of ice cold water.

I couldn't think, couldn't breathe, or even summon a drop of will to push him away. Surrendering to the force pulling us toward each other, I could only exist and feel. Twisting the longer strands of his hair between my fingers, I pulled him closer, chasing his tongue with mine while he explored the cavern of my mouth, leaving no space unturned.

My stomach dipped when he dropped my legs and spun me around so fast that I gasped for air before exhaling loudly when my chest was pressed hard to the door. For a split second, I wondered if Samir would open it to mock me for giving in to my baser needs; but then Dominic wrapped my ponytail around his hand and twisted my face around as much as it would allow before shoving his tongue in my mouth again. All thoughts about the ancient Atua fled my mind.

It was impossible to take a full breath the way I was pressed between the door and Dominic's body, his hard cock wedged between my butt cheeks pulsing in sync with his thrusting tongue. With one hand guiding my head with a firm hold on my hair, he snaked his other hand around my waist and excruciatingly slowly started gliding down my belly.

I gasped in his mouth when his fingers dipped inside the waistband of my pants, popping the buttons open one by one until the tips grazed the soft skin of my belly right above my panties. My ass pressed harder into his erection, encouraging him to hurry up and place his hand where I desperately needed it. There was a pulse between my legs painfully throbbing and begging for relief. But suddenly, the shifter was in no rush to save me from my misery. Oh no. Instead of plunging his fingers inside me, he started making tiny, gentle circles on my skin, driving me insane with need. No amount of wiggling or pressing against him could change his mind or even make him hurry it up. I thought I was losing my hold on reality when I heard a sound, but the vibration moving from his lips to mine told me I wasn't going crazy.

He chuckled.

In his right mind, he chuckled low and growly in my mouth, not pausing the kiss for a second as if my willingness to answer the call my body and the mate bond demanded was funny to him. The familiar burn of anger swirled in the center of my chest, and this time I pushed harder at his body crowding me, not to get closer but to get him off of me.

The arm around my waist tightened painfully, a warning from an alpha male that was attempting to solidify his dominance, but the feline shifter picked the wrong female for that. With a firmer shove, he finally got the message and uncoiled from around me but didn't step back, nor did he remove his mouth from mine. Instead of plundering it with his tongue, he peppered my lips with closed mouth kisses each time our noses connected, forcing me to blink.

"I'm not your enemy," he murmured between pecks,

and I stiffened. He paused kissing me long enough to search my gaze with his for a moment, but he repeated it again after not too long. "I am not your enemy, Brooklyn."

"Could've fooled me." Hating the way I sounded breathless and throaty, I shoved harder to get him to release me. "Get off of me."

"No." Still and unperturbed, he stared unblinkingly at me. "Talk to me."

"I have nothing to say. Now, get off of me." This time I did use my strength instead of the half-assed attempts I'd been giving him. "It's best to keep our distance for now. We need to figure out how to help Alice heal instead of wasting time on nonsense."

"This"—watching me with a raised eyebrow from a couple of steps away where I made him stumble back, he flicked a finger between us—"us, we are the nonsense?"

"She can die at any moment because of this." Mockingly, I flicked my own finger between us, imitating him. It caused a vein to jump on one side of his jaw and his eyes to narrow dangerously at me. "Us, as you like to say. I need to go."

My mouth opened to unleash the torrent of hurtful words that were flooding my brain at that moment but the clearing of a throat from further down the hallway put a stop to it. Later down the road, I would look back at this moment and be eternally grateful for the interruption; but as things were, I turned my glare on Rowen. The witch stood unnaturally still in the middle of the hall. You'd think he appeared there out of thin air.

A muted glow danced all over his tattoos, flickering like the tiny flames on dying embers from his forehead across his nose and down his chin only to disappear into the collar of his T-shirt. Green eyes—so pale it was almost impossible to

see the color of the irises unless you had supernatural sight
—saw way too much for my liking. They looked straight,
not into my gaze, but into my soul. It was so unnerving, I
instinctively took a step toward Dominic, which did not go
unnoticed, much to my annoyance.

The witch made me apprehensive, to say the least.

"Can I help you?" I barked at him snidely and felt
horrible the next second.

It was not his fault that all my nightmares were associ-
ated with witches and those vexatious sigils permanently
marking his skin. If anything, he should've given me hope
with his presence and willingness to help prove that not all
of them were brainwashed puppets with no promise of
redemption. That maybe, just maybe, my mother was not a
villain waiting to strike from the shadows like a snake hiding
in the grass. Alice's smiling face floated tauntingly in my
mind's eye a second before it twisted into a horrified expression and blood gushed between her fingers wrapped around
her neck.

"No," Rowen said softly and moved toward me, his
robes brushing the floor delicately. If I didn't know any
better, I would've thought he was floating. "But I do believe
I can help you."

"I don't need your help." Snapping out of the daze the
swirling robes put me in, I clenched my jaw. "And don't
come anywhere near me." Stabbing a finger in his direction,
I called on all the willpower I had left not to pounce on him,
and rip open his jugular. Something felt off about the situation, but I couldn't put my finger on it. "Rowen, I mean it, I
will kill you if you don't stop."

"You need my help, Brooklyn." Ignoring all the warn-
ings and baring my fangs in his face, he kept gliding toward
me. Dominic, on the other hand, stood there like a lump

just mutely watching. "Allow me to bring you peace." The witch reached for my face, but instead of touching me, he pressed the open veins of his wrists to my lips.

Bitter fluid thick as tar filled my mouth, and I gagged, spitting it out as fast as I could while tears filled my eyes and trickled down my face. Just when I thought I had it all spat out, more poured in and Dominic pressed a hand over my lips, forcing me to swallow it down. It felt like liquid flames burned their way down to my belly, the pain was so intense I had no other option but to pass out.

Darkness claimed me but not before I saw Dominic's blanched face above mine. That only meant one thing. Something was wrong.

Something was horribly wrong.

Place of Torment: Chapter Three

Reality came rushing in through increments a few minutes at a time. Some were calm and collected where I could hear familiar voices of people around me talking in hushed tones, others were from a fantasy movie with distorted faces of monsters, black blood pouring down my throat so bitter I prayed to whoever would listen to allow me to die so I didn't have to endure it anymore. Through it all, there was one constant. Well two if you count the guilt over Alice as a thing.

Dominic's hand held mine. Not helping when I begged him to kill me but not letting go when I felt like I would float away and disappear into nothingness either. Somewhere in the back of my mind a voice was persistent that I needed to wake up. But the moment I tried to open my eyes, searing pain would stab my retinas and I'd promptly pass out after a shrill scream.

"She should've been awake by now if you are telling the truth." A familiar voice growled as I struggled to place it. At first, I thought it was my tormentor and savior from the nearby cage who refused to let me die in peace. But no. This voice was distinctly male, unlike the one reaching my ears from the dark shadows of the cages. Plus, I was on a soft, nicely scented mattress, and not on top of packed dirt soaked with my body fluids.

"Do something." That same deep voice grumbled and the hand holding mine tightened the hold.

"She's coming around." A second voice muttered from right above me. "It's taking longer than I expected but I also have no explanation why we found her collapsed in the hall-way. She seemed okay when I saw her in passing this morning."

"Brooklyn?" Dominic cupped my face and turned it to the sound of his voice. "Can you hear me? Open your eyes, love. Look at me."

A memory filled me of his mouth on mine, his tongue swirling with my tongue, the feel of the slightly raspy texture sending a shiver through my body. Heat bloomed every-where I remembered his hands touching and an embar-rassing moan was ripped from my throat so guttural I felt my face burn in an instant.

"I'd say she's awake." Clearing his throat, the second male that I recognized now as Rowen the witch, couldn't hide his amusement. "I will go check on the human. The potions I brewed keep her barely alive and her situation can go sideways fast. Don't allow Brooklyn to get out of this bed until we are sure she won't collapse again. The last thing we need is the Syndicate getting their hands on her again. If you need me, you can find me there."

A soft click after a moment indicated that Rowen had left while I still gave everything I had to unglue my eyelids. It was as if some invisible power was holding them down and no amount of struggling helped. I was horrified that my heartbeat was still hammering loud enough to wake the dead while the shifter with his acute hearing was looming over me, his face close enough I could feel the heat of his skin from the nearness.

"It's okay." His deep voice reverberated in my chest, sending me on another hormone filled spin down the gutter. "Don't force it, Brooklyn. There is no danger. You can take your time—as long as you need." Callused fingers brushed a strand of hair from my face, the gesture too simple to be felt as intimately as I was feeling it.

I was losing my mind. There was no other explanation for my reaction to Dominic.

I mean the shifter was every female's wet dream, but I had always been able to hold tight control over my hormones and basic needs. Unlike most of my kind, I didn't trust anyone enough to allow them to share my vulnerable moments, be it sex, feeding, or the universe forbid, sleeping next to me. It must be the tainted blood and the prolonged process of healing as it was purged from my system that muddled my brain.

I convinced myself that it was true.

After a while, slowly, my eyes adapted to the light, and I managed to crack them open wide enough to make out Dominic's handsome face. Worry wedged two grooves between his eyebrows, and the five-o-clock shadow I was used to seeing was longer than I remember it. The dark strands of his hair were sticking out every which way, tousled over his forehead as if he'd been running his fingers through it; and the white t-shirt he wore was creased and crinkled, indicating he'd at least slept in it for one night. Disheveled as he was, he had no right to look so damn handsome or irresistible that my fingers were twitching from the need to touch him. Even the dark smudges under his eyes looked good, emphasizing the intense green color of his eyes.

"I've lost my mind." I blurted out, still unable to look away from him.

"Tell me something I don't know." One side of his full lips quirked up and the intensity of his gaze softened when he brushed his knuckles over my cheekbone. "You are awake."

With a herculean effort, I took a deep breath and looked away from his knowing gaze, my eyes latching onto anything around the room so I didn't look like a love-sick fool. The tallboy, the side table, the chair, even the thick curtain bunched up on one side of the window so that the star filled night sky was visible through the glass was a better option than staring at Dominic.

"I guess I should've listened to Samir and rested more instead of keeping vigil over Alice. It's not like I could help her." Uncomfortable as hell, I looked at everything but him. "You found me in the hallway?" Switching the subject away from my friend, which was the main cause of discomfort between Dominic and me, I decided to act dumb.

Ignorance was bliss and I clung to it for dear life. I wasn't pretending that nothing happened between us because my memory was all over the place. The erotic images circling around my head could've been a product of my imagination, and for all I knew he found me crumpled on the floor in front of Alice's room.

Okay, fine, I was fishing for information before making an idiot of myself.

"You don't remember anything before you lost consciousness?" The shifter gave a valiant effort to drill a hole into the side of my face with his intense stare.

"Nope." A headache started developing behind my eyes,

and I rubbed them absentmindedly. "I can't afford to allow this to happen, Dominic. Whatever is left of the Syndicate is searching for us and they'll find us sooner or later. Me dropping like a swatted fly could cost us all our lives."

"No one will harm you anymore." The certainty in his voice made me lock gazes with him. "Rowen made a potion that will speed up the process of purging the tainted blood from your system. I should've found you sooner to ask you to take it, but I got sidetracked. It took even longer because you spat out the first mouthful, and I had to hold you down to force you to drink it."

"You mean Rowen's blood." My face twisted in a grimace, remembering the bitter taste of the thick fluid. "I'd rather keep fainting than drinking that again."

"His blood?" Dominic snarled and I jerked away from him instinctively. "You think I would let the witch feed his blood to my mate?"

Awkward silence filled the space between us, dense enough to be cut with a knife.

"Yes?" I tested his anger tentatively, tensed enough to spring out of bed if he tried to grab me. The expression on his face said he wanted to kill someone, and I was the only person within reach. Call me stupid, but I'd rather be prepared to bounce than test the theory mates can't physically hurt each other.

"It was a potion made of tinctures and herbs," he squeezed out between his grinding teeth and hysterical laughter bubbled up in my chest.

After a few snorts, I couldn't hold it back, and I guffawed in his face before slapping a hand over my mouth. A few more giggles and snorts escaped before I could take a breath and control myself.

"Sorry," I told him from between my fingers, not

trusting myself not to laugh again if I removed my hand. "It must be the potion." More giggles followed.

Much to my surprise, he snorted and joined me, his chuckles slow coming but getting louder by the second.

"I couldn't imagine Rowen's face if he were here when I said I thought he gave me his blood." Wiping at my eyes, I scuttled up the bed to sit up straighter. "Poor witch could've tinkled in his robes seeing that glare you gave me."

"You are definitely testing my control, female." All amusement gone, he looked me up and down as if to assure himself that I was not going to collapse again. "I meant what I said before, Brooklyn. Until now, I let you do things your way but that can no longer be the case. My animal will not let me watch you destroy yourself."

"You think I'm trying to hurt myself?" Appalled by his remark, I recoiled from him.

"I didn't say you do it on purpose, I just said I can't sit back and watch anymore. This is me apologizing for getting in the way of your plans from now on." One shoulder rolled in a half assed shrug.

He didn't look sorry at all.

My mouth opened so I could tell him exactly what I thought about it but scratching at the door got both of our attention. I sat up straighter as Dominic irritably rushed to open the door, his legs eating up the space in two long strides. The wolf stuck his head in as soon as the handle was lowered, and one look at the animal had me jumping out of bed and running toward my friend with my mate hot on my heels.

My mate.

It still gave me goosebumps to even think it.

Place of Torment: Chapter Four

Chicago had a consistent buzz in the air that you got accustomed to regardless of whether you liked it or not. I rejoiced in it every time the soles of my boots brushed the asphalt of the streets as I joined the sea of humans rushing to reach whatever destination they had in mind. It fascinated me to see them hurry to do everything they set out as a goal for the day. They pushed exhaustion aside as if meeting that person, or buying that loaf of bread, would change their world forever or prevent their life from slipping through their fingers before they had time to blink.

So much tension. So much frustration surrounded them as I passed that it was choking me every time I took a deep breath.

"Excuse me," a middle-aged woman muttered as she bumped into me, her shoulder thumping mine in passing, and as my eyes connected with hers, she recoiled from me wide-eyed, the mane of ash blonde strands lifting around her face as if from static. If I didn't know any better, I would've thought she saw the monster I knew I was behind the youthful face and polite expression.

"You're good." I forced a closed-lipped smile and sped up my steps to get away from her. From all of them, actually. It was on me that I didn't spare a second to check my appearance in the mirror before I left as fast, and as quietly, as I could so the shifter wouldn't see me.

Earlier in the day when Dominic and I rushed to Alice to check on her, I realized that I couldn't just sit around and wait for some miracle to happen. I had to go and find a solution that would help bring my friend back to how she was.

First, however, I had to know if the Council was recovering quickly. Or if luck would heal them slowly enough to give me time to help Alice first. In my bloodlust, I'd caused a lot of damage to the Syndicate. Unfortunately, Isiah and Frederic were very good at hiding behind their goons. So, they were out there somewhere in a hole like some roaches waiting for the right moment to strike. It wouldn't do us any good to find help for Alice just so they could snatch her and use her the way they'd used everyone. She would be better off dead if you asked me.

Samir took it upon himself to take care of my friend; so, I decided to address at a later date the issue of the prophecy he shared with me what felt like a lifetime ago. I had no idea if he told Dominic about it as I asked him, and I hoped he didn't share it with Rowen. It made me sound petty, but I still didn't trust the witch.

There was just something about him.

Ducking in a dark alley between two rundown buildings, I waited for the majority of the crowd to dissipate before I decided that stepping out in the open again was safe. It wasn't very late into the evening, the sun having just set an hour or so ago, and the air was still filled with moisture thick enough to drown you. It was sticking to my lungs with each intake of breath, forcing me to put in an effort just so I could breathe. Leaning my head back on the bricks, I closed my eyes, and for the first time, the sigh passing my parted lips sounded as if all the weight in the world just exited my body. It made me so lightheaded I almost missed the sound coming from the second railing of the fire escape across from me. The second a shoe scraped over the metal everything in me stilled, time slowed down to the point that a blink of an eye became eternity.

Whoever it was realized their mistake at the same time, and they froze, not even taking a breath as we both waited to see what the other would do. I immediately knew my stalker was not human. For the predicament they'd found themselves in, their heart rate was too even when it should have been kicking and punching behind their ribcage. It was also impossible for a human to hold their breath that long without passing out. What set me off the most was the lack of scent.

If I were truthful, I expected Dominic to be his usual stubborn self and nip at my heels the second I snuck out of that cursed house. My stomach dropped at the realization that of all things, I was disappointed he respected my wish to be alone. Something he obviously shouldn't have, judging by the fact the person following me got tired of waiting and dropped into the alley nimbly on her toes while I was stuck with my own thoughts and totally forgot she was there.

Yes, it was a she, which was unmistakable when she was in sight.

If that was a Guardian or some mercenary the Council paid to kill me, I would've been long gone without realizing it.

What in all the worlds was the matter with me?

A tiny slip of a female rose up from her crouch, flicking her long dark braid over her shoulder as she did so. Each movement was loaded with self-confidence, that she was exactly where she needed to be and she had the certainty she would be the one that would walk out of the alley, not me. Misguided as her expectations were, I had to give her credit for first impressions and take a second to truly look her up and down.

Given what I had been through and the fact the Council was searching for me dead or alive, I should've been more careful. But supernatural females were rare and precious. For every ten or more males there was one female. Killing one without a second thought would be the greatest crime of them all. And me?

I was not the Council.

I did not kill without reason even if it was a male.

'Tell that to all those souls you sent to the underworld while you were in bloodlust.' A voice in my head mocked me, souring what little decency I had left in me. I refused to stop clinging to it.

"This is pleasantly surprising." The female yet again yanked me from my thoughts, her voice cultured and crisp like she just answered my request to speak to a representative.

Cocking her head to the side, which made her braid swing like a pendulum over her shoulder, she spoke to me conversationally as if we were two friends meeting up for brunch. I couldn't make out her face since she strategically dropped from the fire escape between me and the exit of the alley, placing her back to the light, but there was no mistaking the body of a warrior. The light glow from the street formed an outline around her forcing me to squint in hopes I could catch the color of her eyes which would've helped me recognize her species. Anything would've helped, really.

Unfortunately, I couldn't see a thing, so I figured I'd play her game for the time being.

"It's usually cooler at this hour, but I would agree with you that it's not horribly hot," I answered, and it worked just as I expected it would.

"I was talking about you, not the weather." She tilted her face sideways and laughed. Enough light broke through to show one side of her face. It passed over the rounded cheekbone, quite long lashes, and the glint of her irises. Her eyes shimmered and brightened for a split second to give her away as a demon.

Taken by surprise, I flinched back, something she didn't miss. All humor left her, and she stiffened, slightly bending her knees in preparation for an attack. My body reacted accordingly, moving my feet slightly apart and relaxing my shoulders so I could move fast if I needed to.

Everything about the situation was off. The Council sent a demon after me? And since I was not trying my best to remove my clothing, she was not a succubus sent to drain the life out of me. I'd heard stories about them but never had the opportunity of meeting one in person. Male or female, it was a very unpleasant way of dying, I'd been told.

"You're a demon," I blurted out, opting for the truth.

"And you are an Atua." She countered, neither accusing me nor judging me for it.

"My guess is the Council sent you to hunt me down, so let's get this over with. I have places to be." With a roll of my shoulders, I took a step toward her.

"They did hire me, but I didn't accept the job so I could kill you." Lifting both hands to her sides, palms up, she countered my movement by stepping back and maintaining the distance between us. "I've been following you for the last few weeks and maintaining my distance because I didn't think you would be willing to stop for a moment and talk. Everything I've learned about you is that you kill first, you check who and what you separated from the land of the living later." Slowly, purposely she turned her body so that I could fully see her. "I thought I was wasting my time trying to chat to tell you the truth."

Chocolate color skin glistened in the light, beautifully outlining the muscles of her toned arms. A leather vest was wrapped around her torso ending an inch above the waistband of the skin-tight leather pants which looked spray-painted over the legs. There was nothing apart from her long braid that anyone could grab and use against her in a fight. It spoke of experience and promised death to any opponent.

Her demeanor, the tone of her voice, her heart rate and her body language did the right thing though and told me she was speaking the truth. Her only mistake was admitting she accepted a job from the Council. There was not a soul in this world or any other that would risk double-crossing them by agreeing to something and not following through.

She was still turned, her upper body slightly back and to the side, an awkward enough position that would work to my advantage when I struck, and I took the chance. Swiping my foot in a wide arc, I took her feet from under her, following it through with an uppercut punch that caught her chin and whipped her head back. A satisfying crack bounced off of the dirty walls around us, breaking the silence, and I smiled at her grunt when the air left her lungs the second her back hit the ground.

With surprising speed, she was up and backing me into

a corner, her smaller size giving her an advantage. My offensive attack turned into defense, and I hoped I didn't make a mistake of underestimating the demon. My arm hurt every time I deflected her punches, and my shins were bruising from the strength of her kicks. We were moving so fast dust was picking up and forming tiny tornadoes at our feet but neither one of us was backing down. And that was when it happened. For the first time in my life that I could remember, someone managed to best me in a fight.

The female performed a side kick and threw both her hands in front of her the second her feet touched the ground so she was facing me. Red threads of magic burst from her palms and hit me like a ton of bricks at the center of my chest, punching all the air out of me. Searing pain spread through my entire body, and I had no time to think when it knocked me out. The last thought I had was the regret that I would never see Dominic again to tell him how much he meant to me and that I was sorry that I was so damaged that I couldn't be what he needed.

Darkness swallowed me whole.

Grab your copy…
vinci-books.com/placeoftorment

About the Author

Maya Daniels, USA Today Bestselling and multi-award-winning supernatural suspense author, is a fun-loving woman with many talents.

She traveled the world, gaining life experiences that helped her career as an investigative journalist, as well as her storytelling. Maya writes compelling tales of magic, mythical creatures, loyalty, and life-changing friendships with snarky female characters—much like herself.

Her travels have taken her to Europe, Africa, Asia, Australia, and America. Born with her feet in motion, she currently resides in Ohio, spinning her next epic story that you will not want to put down.

Her biggest 'sins' are her love of chocolate and coffee—through an IV drip! One to never sit still, Maya practices Reiki healing, different types of martial arts, reads about the arcane, talks to furry creatures more than humans, picks up a sledgehammer for home improvement, and travels with her fated mate, seeking her own adventures.